To

Christopher & Jan,

from one cowboy and
his sidekick to
another and his !!

Love,

Derek

Feb '00.

Top Gun For Hire

Top Gun For Hire

DEREK TAYLOR

A Black Horse Western

ROBERT HALE · LONDON

© Derek Taylor 1999
First published in Great Britain 1999

ISBN 0 7090 6489 6

Robert Hale Limited
Clerkenwell House
Clerkenwell Green
London EC1R 0HT

The right of Derek Taylor to be identified as
author of this work has been asserted by him
in accordance with the Copyright, Designs and
Patents Act 1988.

Photoset in North Wales by
Derek Doyle & Associates, Mold, Flintshire.
Printed and bound in Great Britain by
WBC Book Manufacturers Limited, Bridgend.

For Annie 'Oakley' White who bit the dust too soon but who, unafraid, rode the trail doin' what came naturally.

ONE

The Lazy Day Saloon was busy. Three young men, strangers in town and low-life of the usual, lawless, western kind, were propped up against the bar drinking. They were egging one another on to do something each one of them would rather have shied away from, but which now severally they had no choice but to see through. One of them had recognized John Thirsk. He'd pointed him out to the others, and they'd all agreed it would enhance their reputations to cut him down to size.

John Thirsk was finishing his last shot of rye whiskey. He'd enjoyed a few drinks and passing conversation with friends and neighbours, but now the atmosphere was becoming rowdy and he was thinking it was time he returned to the hotel in town. The three men at the other end of the bar were getting noisier and he had caught snippets of the things they were saying to one another. He smelled trouble.

He emptied his glass and, putting it down on the bar, caught the eye of the bartender.

'Have another, Mr Thirsk?' the bartender asked.

'I don't think so, Mike,' John Thirsk replied. 'Think I'll be heading on home.'

Three young hotheads had other ideas about that. As John Thirsk began to walk away from the bar, one of them called out his name. Slowly, he turned to face them. Seeing him do so, the greater part of the bravado went out of the three young men. Most of the company carousing in the Lazy Day had not yet noticed what was starting, and the hum and hubbub continued at a high level. But those who had noticed tried to put some safe footage between themselves and what was starting.

John Thirsk said nothing in reply to the man who had called out his name. He had learned from the past there was little to be gained from trying to talk sense to delinquent young bucks. Eyeballing them usually achieved more. It undid further already shaky nerves.

The three men looked from one to the other, asking without words who was going to be the one to draw first. One of them had always been more reckless than the others and reckoned himself to be pretty fast with a gun. John Thirsk was old now, he persuaded himself, old enough anyway to have lost the edge. His friends were either side of him. He knew they'd be expecting him to make the first move. And he was right. They did look at him, waiting for him to indicate what they should do next. His bladder was full from all the drinking, and he began to feel it was time he left to take a leak. Such a feeling of urgency dictated his next move. In a flash his gun was out, followed quickly by those of his sidekicks. But not quickly enough. Three shots rang out, all of which left the barrel of John Thirsk's Colt Peacemaker smoking. Three young men lay dying, one of them in a spreading puddle of his own urine.

TWO

John Thirsk stepped out of the saloon and looked up and down Main Street. Behind him he had left mayhem. Three men dead. Many more standing in stunned silence. *So it goes*, John Thirsk thought, as he turned left and walked in the direction of the town's only decent hotel. It was run by Rosalee, the buxomest brunette this side of St Louis.

His spurs jangled as he walked. His step was steady. Some men felt shaky after a gunfight, but not John Thirsk. There were always people passing by who thought they could take him on. His reputation dogged him. He was the man who had bettered even Wyatt Earp, whose famed Colt Peacemaker had served only the law. Every long-rider in the West had heard of him and reckoned, luck being on their side, they could out-draw him.

In the hotel bar Rosalee was standing between two men engaged in what was obviously pleasant or playful – and probably both – conversation. She

11

didn't immediately extract herself when she saw John Thirsk walk in. She just let him see that his entrance had not gone unnoticed. For his part, he simply sauntered up to the bar and ordered his usual.

'Sure thing,' smiled the bartender.

'Heard you were bothered again,' said Rosalee, appearing beside him as he downed his second shot of whiskey. She looked as lovely as always. Buxom and senuous. All woman. All desirable.

'Yeah,' was all he said in reply.

'They'll learn one day,' she said, matter-of-factly.

'Yeah,' he said again.

Rosalee stroked his cheek. He smiled appreciatively. She turned to go back to her customers, but not before giving him a look of love that put his spirits back on top of the world.

Three days later there was another young man in town seeking out John Thirsk. He found him in the Lazy Day Saloon.

'Are you John Thirsk?' the young man asked. He was barely out of his teens, though he was tall and dark in a manly sort of way. On his left side was a big iron.

As Thirsk turned to face him he was on his guard. Experience had taught him to be so. Looking at the young man, he was surprised not to find him standing tense and ready to draw. He

12

also noted that the young man had a face that was strikingly familiar.

'Who's asking?' he said, looking the young man firmly in the eye.

There was no suggestion of a challenging look in the young man's eye, and Thirsk was relieved to think that his enquiry was not going to lead to more work for the town's undertaker.

'Frank Butler's son,' replied the young man.

Frank Butler – that was it, Thirsk thought, as he turned to get a better look at the young man. That was whose face he might have been looking into. The young man standing in front of him might have been broader and altogether thicker, but that square chin and long neck were Frank Butler's all right. The eyes, too. Even the moustache. And the hat. Frank was never seen in any other.

'And what might Frank Butler's son be wanting with me?' John Thirsk asked, downing the last of his drink and shoving his glass in the direction of the bartender.

The bartender, like everyone else in the saloon, had stopped what he was doing and held his breath when Frank Butler's son had made his approach to John Thirsk. Seeing there was going to be no trouble, he and everyone else relaxed and the saloon began again to fill with the buzz of conversation. The bartender refilled John Thirsk's glass and put it down in front of him.

'Pa told me before he died if ever we was faced with more trouble than we could handle I was to find you and ask for help.'

Frank Butler dead? John Thirsk thought for a moment and then turned to face the young man. He hadn't seen Frank Butler for more than five years. Last he heard of him he'd settled somewhere in Arkansas. Saved most of what they'd made in rewards way down in Texas for precisely that purpose and got himself a small farm. A farm to replace the one the railroad had ridden right through and scattered his family from.

'Well you'd best sit down and tell me all about it, son.'

Jesse Butler sat down. He'd been looking for John Thirsk all summer and was relieved to have found him at last. The tale he had to tell was not a happy one. He accepted the drink he was offered, and began to tell his story. John Thirsk listened.

He learned that Frank Butler had also been plagued by young guns who thought they had something to prove. Only one of them, or so it was presumed, had jumped out on Frank and wounded him so badly that after a few weeks he died. That had been a year ago back in Walnut Ridge, Arkansas. Frank had acquired a farm of seven hundred acres and had been making a living. The ground was good for cotton, and they'd kept a few head of beef and dairy cattle. The farm

14

had passed down to Frank's widow, Jesse and a younger brother, John. Or so they thought, until one of their neighbours, a rich landowner called Milton, had come along and laid claim to it.

'On what grounds?' John Thirsk asked. His mind rushed back to Texas, where he and Frank Butler had played a big part in making the world a safer place for settlers, only to find the terror of outlaws replaced by the tyranny of political outlaws, whose methods were no less cruel, no less summary.

He'd been saddened to hear his old sidekick was dead, and from the disease that plagued anyone who found himself with a legendary reputation for handling a gun: the bravado of young guns. Jesse was so much a chip off the old block that he couldn't help but warm to him. Had he been born into the same times as him and Frank, no doubt he'd have followed exactly the same path as they were forced to take. Wasn't he even now looking to face head-on a problem that most settlers ran away from?

'Well,' Jesse explained, 'Pa bought the farm off a man who said he'd won it in a game of poker. Milton says that it hadn't been anyone's farm to wager in a card game. That it was never an owned farm, only a let one, and one let by him.'

'Why didn't this come to light before?'

'Because, this man Milton says, Pa had a lawyer forge a set of deeds which fooled everyone.'

'Well, didn't Milton notice that no one was paying rent on the farm? I mean, you rent out farms to make money, don't you?' asked John Thirsk.

'We ain't ever got a proper answer to those kind of obvious questions, and in the meantime Milton's men have been ruining our crops and stealing our cattle. The sheriff don't do nothing about it 'cause he's in Milton's pay, and the rest of the folks around about are too scared. Most of them have been run off their farms by Milton anyways. Ma, Johnny and me have been doing our best, but I'm afraid we're all gonna get killed before Milton's done. Unless, that is, you can do something to help, Mr Thirsk. Pa said you would, if ever there was a problem too big for us to handle. And this sure is one.'

John Thirsk knew he owed it to Frank Butler to try and do something for the family he'd left behind. Frank had risked his own life more than once to save his. They'd got into a shoot-out after thwarting a gang robbing a bank. He'd been wounded and fallen, and Frank had walked into a storm of lead to save him from what would have been certain death.

'There must be something more to this man Milton's claim than suddenly missing the rent he reckons he's due,' John Thirsk remarked, thinking out loud. 'If it was just that, he'd be waiting for the law-courts to decide the matter. Is there anything you can think of?'

Jesse Butler's brow furrowed as he tried to think.

'Well, I have thought about that,' he said, 'but there don't appear to be no other reason. We got plenty of water on our lands, but so has Milton. Other than that I don't know what it can be.'

There was a silence while the two men pondered the matter. Jesse was hoping Thirsk would accompany him back to the farm, while Thirsk was wondering how Rosalee would take it.

'Will you come and help, Mr Thirsk?' Jesse asked at last.

Thirsk's right hand went naturally to his gun. He hadn't used it for more than self-defence in over three years. He was still quick, he knew, but did he have the mind for it? He reckoned he had to have. Frank would have done it for him and his, of this he had no doubt. Turning to tell Frank Butler's boy that, yes, he would come, he hoped Rosalee would understand.

THREE

Rosalee did not like it but she knew Thirsk had to go. His honour demanded it of him. She knew, too, that he hated to leave her and it consoled her greatly. Poplar Bluff was a peaceful town, and she had no fear that trouble for her and her girls would follow his departure. Besides, people knew of his past, and while hotheads might chance their luck with him, nobody else did or would. His reputation was all the protection she needed.

On the evening of their last night together, John Thirsk watched as Rosalee moved amongst the gathered company of the hotel. Her long, flowing silk skirts crowned with a bustle and close-fitting bodice trimmed with lace gave her a femininity and beauty rare in these parts. About her neck she wore a scarlet ribbon choker bejewelled in the front with a large topaz. Her auburn curls fell freely about her forehead. Every man wanted her, but she was his and his alone, he knew he could trust to this.

They had fallen in love the first time their eyes met in a small town in mid-Texas. He was a personage to reckon with then, but it was to her ever after that he brought the fruits of law-enforcement. When there was enough money in hand, she finally went ahead of him and settled in Poplar Bluff where they built the hotel that was intended to be his future, but more importantly, their home.

It was a home he had no desire to leave now. He felt it all the more deeply as he waited for the woman he loved to signal to him she could retire for the night. His Colt Peacemaker was still in its holster. He was the only person permitted to wear a gun in the White Horse Hotel. Contemplating the early departure he'd have to make the next morning, he fingered the yellowed ivory grips of his gun. Without it slung about his hips, he felt naked. Frank Butler's son was already in bed. It was near midnight. Time he turned in, he reckoned. Knocking back the last of two fingers of red-eye, he pushed back his chair and got up. Just in time to catch Rosalee's eye. He lifted his head upwards to indicate he was going to retire. She mouthed that she would be there in five minutes.

Three days of hard riding later, John Thirsk and Jesse Butler rode into Walnut Ridge. It was a one-horse town, but set to grow as cotton farming in the locality began to get into its stride.

20

'How far d'you say it is to your place from here?'
John Thirsk asked Jesse as they walked their
horses down Main Street.

'Some fifteen miles,' replied Jesse, looking to
see if there was anyone he knew stepping out on
the plankwalks that he could ask about Ma and
Johnny.

'Well, reckon we oughtta stay here the night.
Talk to the Sheriff. See how the land is lying.'

'Reckon we could,' agreed Jesse, 'though I sure
am anxious to know how Ma and Johnny is.'

'Happen there's someone here that can tell you,'
Thirsk said. 'Know of anywheres decent round
here to get a meal and a drink?'

They were in the middle of town by now. Jesse
looked at the wooden, square-faced buildings that
made up Main Street. One of them was
O'Mahone's Saloon.

'That's as good a place as any,' Jesse said, pointing to it.

They tied up their horses in front of it and went
in. Pushing through a pair of bat-wings, Thirsk
entered the saloon and led the way to the bar. The
place was empty save for a bartender polishing
glasses behind a long mahogany bar. He acknowledged the two men with a nod as they came in. He
didn't know Jesse, as O'Mahone's was not a place
Jesse's father would have liked him to frequent.
Besides which he was still young, and rarely came
to town except with Ma and Jim, one of the Negro

workers, to buy provisions. So, to the bartender, the two men were strangers in town.

'What can I get you?'

Jesse decided he wouldn't have a drink yet. He was anxious to find someone who might be able to tell him something of his folks. He said as much to John Thirsk.

'OK. I'll be waiting here,' John Thirsk said, pouring himself two fingers of red-eye from the bottle the bartender had fetched for him. He took the bottle and his glass and sat down at a table.

Jesse went straight to the general store where his family were well known. Milton was still being pushy, but otherwise things were no different, they told him. Or weren't up until a week ago, which was when they last saw Johnny and Jim who'd come to town to buy provisions.

'Well, that's something,' John Thirsk said when he heard. 'Maybe your father's title has been proven and my trip's been unnecessary.'

'It'll be a miracle if it has,' Jesse remarked. 'There were no papers that we or anyone could find. Nothing lodged anywhere.'

'Either way,' concluded John Thirsk, emptying his glass, 'the sheriff's the next call. Where will we find him?'

'His office is just up Main Street.'

'Well, no time like the present. Let's get it over with,' John Thirsk said, getting up.

He went to the bar and asked the bartender

how much he owed him. Peering over to the table where they'd sat and seeing the bottle half-empty, the bartender told him a dollar. Taking out a silver coin, John Thirsk flicked it to him.

'You're strangers in town, aren't you?' the bartender remarked as they turned to leave.

'I am,' John Thirsk said over his shoulder, 'but Jesse here owns a farm in these parts. I'm here to prove it, if need be,' he added, thinking it did no harm to let it be known. After all, bartenders always knew everyone's business. This one might just as well know his. That way Milton would soon get to know it too.

FOUR

They found Sheriff Turner in his office. He was a
big man with a slightly shifty look. Looking up
when he saw them, he said to Jesse, 'Jesse, boy,
you're back! It's been a few months. I was only
saying to your ma the other day—'

'Yes, sir,' replied Jesse respectfully. Knowing
Sheriff Turner was in Milton's pay, he didn't trust
him and had no liking for him. 'This is John
Thirsk, a friend of Pa's.'

John Thirsk and Sheriff Turner eyeballed one
another, Sheriff Turner suspiciously and Thirsk
contemptuously, remembering all of what Jesse
had told him. And also because he knew the sort
of man Turner was. He could read him like a book,
having come up against enough of his opportunis-
tic kind before. Sheriff Turner got up and held out
a hand to John Thirsk, who ignored it.

'I hope you'll like our little town,' Sheriff Turner
remarked, awkwardly taking his hand back.

'I don't reckon on being here long enough to get to know it,' John Thirsk answered. 'I'll come straight to the point, Sheriff; what's all this about this man called Milton laying claim to Jesse here and his widowed Ma's inheritance?'

'Yeah, well that is unfortunate. But it's in the hands of lawyers and it's nothing much to do with me,' replied Sheriff Turner, returning to his seat and making himself a cigarette. He offered his makings to Jesse and John Thirsk, but they both declined.

'That's not what Jesse here tells me. In fact, he tells me that Milton and his men have been terrorizing his family and that you ain't done much about it.' Sheriff Turner moved uneasily in his seat.

'Now lookey here, Mr Thirsk,' replied Sheriff Turner, now visibly squirming in his seat. 'I've done my job there and I ain't found any proof yet that Milton and his men are behind any of what's been going on at the Butlers' Farm. Milton's gone to law, and until I have proof that he's trying other methods to enforce his claim to Horseshoe Farm there's nothing I can do.'

Jesse stood looking uneasy, but John Thirsk was standing firm and looking Sheriff Turner menacingly in the eye. He had enough experience to know he was lying.

'Well, let me tell you something, Sheriff, I've been told different and if what I've been told turns

26

out to be true our friend Mr Milton will find the law little help to him.'

'We don't want no trouble round here, Mr Thirsk. Mrs Butler knows I've done all I can to find out who's been ruining their crops and running off their cattle, and she ain't said otherwise to me or anyone else. Now you can investigate all you want but if you come up with anything, you come into town and tell me. I don't hold with anyone taking the law into their own hands. You just remember that.'

'Unless their name has got "big man" written all over it,' John Thirsk sneeringly replied.

Sheriff Turner suddenly realized what he was up against and he was not a happy man.

'Well, you can tell your big man,' John Thirsk continued, 'that the little people around here ain't alone no more.'

John Thirsk said no more but simply stood tall, hand on gun, staring the sheriff right in the eye. He kept his penetrating gaze on him for what seemed to Sheriff Turner like an eternity, and then turned and walked out of his office.

'Sheriff,' was all Jesse said, tipping his Stetson and following John Thirsk out of the office.

'You remember what I said now, Mr Thirsk, and Jesse, you make sure that he does. I won't have it any other way.'

Neither John Thirsk nor Jesse answered this last remark of the sheriff's. Instead they walked off in the direction of the town's only hotel, where they aimed to spend the night.

One hour later Sheriff Turner was walking into Milton's ranch house. Milton was surprised to see him. He was standing with his back to a blazing fire and was drawing on a large Cuban cigar when Turner appeared.

'Why, Sheriff—' he began.

'This is no social call,' Sheriff Turner interrupted him. 'Jesse Butler has returned with a friend of his father's. A mean looking sonofabitch. He was making threats.'

'What sort of threats?' Milton asked. He was a short, squat man with a bullish neck. In five years he had turned a large farm into a hundred thousand-acre spread. He despised what he called the 'little men', and was ruthless in the way he brushed them aside to fulfill his own ambitions.

'He said that if he finds out you've been harassing the Butlers, you'd have him to answer to.'

'And that's a threat,' smirked Milton, rocking on his heels and dragging on his cigar.

'He meant it, Mr Milton,' Sheriff Turner emphasized.

'Yeah, well, I can make a few threats of my own. The Butlers are all but finished. I think it's time we enforced that notice to quit. Let's see what this friend of Frank Butler deceased has to say about that.'

'Do you think that's wise, Mr Milton?' Sheriff Turner asked. 'I mean, your claim has still not been proved.'

'Sheriff, my claim has not been disproved either. None of my claims have ever been. This one will not turn out to be any different.'

'There is one difference,' Sheriff Turner warned him. 'The Butlers have proved to be more stubborn than most. And no one's ever brought in outside help before. Maybe we should wait for the courts to decide.'

Milton said nothing for a moment. He eyed Sheriff Turner with a concentrated stare. It made him feel threatened and reminded him that what Milton demanded, Milton usually got. In these parts he was king. When Milton next spoke what he said did not surprise Turner.

'Burn their barns. Tonight.'

FIVE

John Thirsk and Jesse rode out of Walnut Ridge at just gone nine the next morning. They were watched from his office window by Sheriff Turner. He was bleary-eyed from lack of sleep, but this was not obvious to John Thirsk or Jesse as they rode down the middle of Main Street. Catching a glimpse of him at his window, John Thirsk thought of how many men like him he and Jesse's father had put in their graves. No point in warning this one of that, he knew. Vermin like him would never heed it.

He knows, was the Sheriff's only thought as he watched John Thirsk ride by. He knows.

John Thirsk and Jesse rode their American breeds hard. The tracks Jesse took them along skirted what was nearly all Milton land. Not long ago most of this land had been forest, but the trees had been cleared and now it was all under cotton. There were new homesteaders coming all the time, near penniless and making huge sacri-

31

fices to lay claim to and develop their one hundred and sixty acres. Milton would not be happy until he had all this land under his belt.

John Thirsk hated these robber landowners. He had seen them in action all over the West, stealing the hopes and dreams of the little people of the old world and their descendants. People who had fled the evil tyrannies of the old masters, only to find themselves falling victim to the new. Small or great, here was a robber baron now. But he was determined – Milton was not going to steal even one boll of cotton from Frank Butler's farm without paying a very heavy price for it.

They rode on, making good ground. Jesse was in front and had just called over his shoulder to John Thirsk to tell him there was not much further to go when they noticed a cloud of smoke in the distance. Jesse reined in his horse and stopped. John Thirsk followed suit.

'Looks like our place,' Jesse groaned.

'Are you sure?' John Thirsk asked.

'No, but it sure looks like it,' was Jesse's reply, his tone full of concern. 'Come on,' he added, digging his unspurred boot heels into his horse's flanks and setting off at a gallop.

John Thirsk wasn't far behind. The closer they got to the farm, the more convinced Jesse was that it was their place. He just hoped Ma and Johnny were all right. They arrived to find them not hurt but angry and distressed. Jesse jumped off his horse almost before it had stopped. Ma, Johnny and the workers were standing looking at the smouldering ruins of the barn.

'Jesse!' Mary Butler exclaimed on seeing him. 'You're back son, safe and sound.'

'Yeah, Ma, but what's been happening here?'

'The animals set up a terrible row in the early hours of the morning and woke us all. The barn was ablaze. We managed to get the animals out but you can see that we couldn't save the barn.'

'Anyone hurt?'

'No, thank God,' said Johnny. 'Who's this with you?'

Johnny was younger than Jesse but not much smaller. He was blond, taking after his mother.

'This is John Thirsk. You know, Pa's friend,' replied Jesse. 'Mr Thirsk, meet Ma and Johnny.'

John Thirsk acknowledged them both with a nod of his head and a touch of his hat. 'Was it an accident?' he asked.

'I don't think so. More'n likely Milton,' Johnny replied, wiping his face with an already blackened neckerchief.

'Now we don't know that, Johnny,' Ma said. She was a woman of over thirty, tall and straight with her hair tied up in a bun.

'Oh, Ma, you know it was him. The barn was set ablaze in half-a-dozen different places. Fires like

33

that don't start accidentally,' Johnny insisted.

'Anybody see anything?' John Thirsk asked, getting down off his horse.

'Jim here reckons he heard something like the sound of horses making a getaway,' Johnny replied, pointing in the direction of a large, stocky Negro standing close by.

'Is that right?' Jessie asked.

'Sure thing, boss. I knowed it was hosses.'

Jesse turned and looked at John Thirsk.

'It was a warning to me, son,' John Thirsk said, 'but I don't scare that easily.'

Jesse looked reassured. 'Any of the cotton in there?' he asked.

'All of it,' replied Johnny. 'At least of what was left after Milton's men burnt the fields, and that weren't much.'

'OK,' said John Thirsk. 'Jesse, reckon you and I are gonna make a call on Milton. How far's his spread from here?'

'Ain't we gonna ride into town and tell the sheriff?' Johnny asked as he and the others surveyed the charred ruins of the barn.

'There ain't no point in that, Johnny. We all know he's in the pay of Milton,' Jesse replied. 'He'd just say it was an act of God, a bolt of lightning or some such fool thing.'

'Jesse, I asked you how far Milton's spread is from here and you ain't given me an answer.'

'It's all around us, Mr Thirsk.'

'Jesse, stop calling me Mister and start calling me John.'

'All right, John,' Jesse replied, feeling all of a sudden much more of an adult, 'his spread is all around us, but his ranch is a few hours' ride away.'

'I reckon it's time I paid him a visit, don't you?' John Thirsk said. 'And there ain't no time like the present.'

'Do you reckon that's wise?' Jesse asked.

'If this is his work, and we know it is, then I don't see we got any choice. What about the other homesteaders around here? Is he trying to run them off their land, too?'

'He's done it, mostly,' said Johnny. 'We're about the only ones left, and we can't hold out for much longer now that the cotton crop's been burned.'

'You ever fired that gun of yours, Jesse?' John Thirsk asked.

'Only at tin cans, but I was taught to shoot by Pa.'

'Well, your Pa knew how to handle a gun. Let me see you shoot,' John Thirsk said, looking about for a good spot.

They got some cans and set them up a few hundred yards from the house. Jesse shot well, very well, considering, but John Thirsk told him there was more to looking after yourself than being able to hit a target at a few paces.

'I know that, John,' he said. 'But I don't see as I've got time or the opportunity to learn, except by following you.'

'I guess you're right, son. And you are your father's son. That is pretty obvious to me by the way you shoot,' John Thirsk replied, remembering how lightning-quick Frank Butler was at picking off anyone who raised a gun to him from any direction.

'I can shoot, too,' said Johnny. He was just a kid but believed he was enough of a man to stand tall in any fight.

'Yeah, Johnny, but you oughtta stay here and look after Ma,' Jesse answered him, using tact where he knew anything else would amount to put-down. 'Someone's gotta do it and you're the only one.'

Johnny wasn't convinced but to argue would have been equal to disregarding his mother's need and he didn't want to risk that.

'Your brother's right,' echoed John Thirsk. 'Any of your men fire a gun?'

'Jim's good with a rifle. Pa also showed him a thing or two.'

'Has he got one?'

'Yeah, a Winchester. They got two or three between them.'

'Reckon you can trust 'em?' John Thirsk asked.

'Sure thing. They coulda left any time they wanted, but they reckon Pa was good to them and they ain't leaving till we do,' Jessie answered.

'Yeah, your Pa never did hold with slavery, said the South got what it deserved for trying to keep its slaves in bondage. He was a good man,' John Thirsk said.

Jessie and Johnny looked at each other mournfully. They didn't know much about their father's past except that it had been colourful. It broke their hearts when he was gunned down, and they hadn't yet got over their grief.

'Ain't you gonna stop and have something to eat first?' Mary asked.

'Reckon not, ma'am, it's getting late in the day and we don't want to be riding in the dark,' John Thirsk replied.

'Well at least have a coffee. There's a pot on the stove,' Mary added.

John Thirsk agreed to that. He was thirsty from the trail, and hungry, but after one mug of coffee he and Jesse were back in their saddles. They rode hard into the day until they came to within a short distance of Milton's spread. John Thirsk had kept alert, observing the lay of the land and watching out for bushwhackers as they went along. He knew that Milton would know by now of his existence. He knew too that he would stop at nothing to take the Butler farm. He wasn't about to make it easy for him by allowing himself to be picked off on the trail by some sharp-shooter.

They reined in their horses on a bit of high ground less than a quarter of a mile from Milton's ranch. Looking down on a substantial house with some of the charms of a southern plantation edifice, John Thirsk asked himself how well protected and prepared for any unwelcome visitors Milton would be. Not very, he reckoned. Men like Milton were arrogant. To his way of thinking his enemy was weak and without resource, that is, already defeated. He would therefore assume he had nothing to fear from anyone anywhere in the county.

'You stick close to me, Jesse, and keep your eyes peeled,' John Thirsk said, turning to the young and as yet untried innocent at his side. 'And don't draw unless and until someone draws on you, or I draw. Got that?'

Jesse looked at John Thirsk, his stomach full of nerves. He'd never yet been in a gunfighter's shoes, and fear gripped him hard.

'Don't worry about me,' he bravely said in reply.

'I ain't. You're a son of Frank's, ain't you? But I know what it can be like. I've done it enough times,' John Thirsk said, gritting his teeth and looking earnest. He spurred his horse and set off at a trot. Jesse followed suit.

As they neared Milton's ranch they could see there was work afoot to extend it and make it even more palatial than it already was. It sickened both Thirsk and Jesse to know how he'd come by the wealth to afford it. Milton was on the steps of the house as they rode up to it. His foreman was with him. They were going into the building, but stopped when they heard horses approaching. Jesse and Thirsk drew up.

'Yes, gentlemen, what can we do for you?' Milton said, as cool as if their arrival was by invitation. He already knew who Jesse was and guessed who the stranger with him was.

Neither Jesse nor John Thirsk answered Milton's question. Thirsk was studying what in his mind was the enemy, while Jesse was simply taking his lead. The foreman, a tall, swarthy looking tough guy, was wearing a pair of Frontier Colts. He looked mean enough to use them without much provocation. Milton, bull-necked, stocky and shorter, looked self-possessed and commanding.

'Well,' the foreman, whose name was O'Leary, said at last. 'Ain't you gonna answer Mr Milton's question?'

Jesse looked at John Thirsk.

'You're Frank Butler's son, aren't you?' Milton said. 'You've come, I take it, to tell me you're all loaded up and ready to go.'

'He ain't,' interrupted John Thirsk.

'And who might you be?' Milton asked, knowing full well he was the man Sheriff Turner had told him about.

'Who I am don't matter. What does,' said Thirsk, 'is what I've come to say.'

'Which is?' Milton asked.

'No one is leaving the Butlers' farm. The whole family, or what's left of it, is staying put. And if you, or any of your men, step one foot on their land, it'll be the last step you, or they, ever take.'

'And what about my legal claim? Has Jesse or his mother bothered to tell you about that?'

'I ain't interested in that. That's something for the lawyers to sort out, and while they're doing so the farm remains the property of the Butlers. That is the law. But you seem to view things differently.'

There was a moment's silence while the men on either side eyeballed one another. O'Leary was itching to let Jesse and John Thirsk have it, while Milton was taking on board just what he could see he was now up against. Trouble with a capital 'T' was what it had become.

'This ain't your fight,' Milton said at last. 'Why don't you leave while you still can?'

Jesse stirred uneasily in his saddle. O'Leary's hands moved to hover over his .45s. John Thirsk went for his Peacemaker. Less than a second later O'Leary was lying dead on the steps.

'I told you,' Milton gasped after a stunned silence, 'this is not your fight.'

'It is now,' John Thirsk said. 'And you've been warned, Milton.'

To Milton's great relief he re-holstered his gun. Other men who heard the shot began to appear. Milton raised his hands in a gesture that told them to leave things alone. Jesse looked on, horror-struck. John Thirsk had just killed a man in cold blood. Was he going to kill another?

'Look, Mister whoever-you-are. This is not the way,' Milton said.

'It's been your way, Milton, up until now. You know what'll follow if there's any more of it.'

John Thirsk stared long and hard into Milton's face and deep into his psyche. He found nothing but an empty shell of a soul there. Such men, he knew, sought to make good their deficiencies by feeding on the vulnerabilities of ordinary decent folk. And he knew they were so wanton in their need that only a lightning strike could halt them in their tracks. Knowing he had delivered one to Milton, he turned his horse around slowly and began to take his leave. Ten men had their eyes on him. Some of them were holding rifles, others hand-guns. One word from Milton and they would have let rip. But Milton said nothing. His concern suddenly was for his own life. The man was fast. Lightning fast. Too fast for anyone there to take on. Another time, another place, and perhaps the odds would not be so heavily stacked against them. As some of his men looked at him with pleading eyes, he let John Thirsk and Jesse Butler ride away.

'Johnstone,' he turned and snapped at one of the men when John Thirsk and Jesse Butler were far enough out of sight. 'You've been promoted. You're foreman. Now go to town and find Turner. Tell him I want him out here now.'

Johnstone, another big man, only fair and lean, jumped to. Milton stepped over O'Leary without giving him a second glance and walked up the steps into his house. As he went he pulled a handkerchief out of a pocket and mopped a wet and burning brow.

Johnstone found Sheriff Turner in his office. When told what had happened, the sheriff said he'd been expecting something like it to occur. He didn't relish trying to arrest John Thirsk, and was relieved that the first thing he had to do was to see Milton. Leaving a deputy in charge, he got on his horse and rode back to Milton's spread with Johnstone.

'I warned you, Mr Milton,' were the words he greeted Milton with.

Milton filled him in with the details of exactly what had happened. Then he said, 'Well, Turner, somehow or other you got to go and get him arrested and hanged, before things get out of hand.' Turner didn't look too happy about it. 'There are men like him wreaking havoc all over the West,' Milton continued, 'and they gotta be stopped. He's fast but he took O'Leary by surprise. Next time we'll be ready for him and he won't find it quite so easy.'

'Maybe we best try and take him at the Butlers' farm. We could surround the place,' Sheriff Turner declared.

'Take him where you like,' Milton said, 'only take him. And the Butler boy, too. Dead or alive. If alive, string 'em both up. I want that farm, Turner, and I aim to have it. I got geologists coming from the East any day now and I don't want the Butlers getting to know what's beneath their land.'

A few months previously Milton had sent for analysis some unusual-looking rock he had begun to notice was in abundance everywhere. He was told it was bauxite, from which aluminum, the new metal, was made. If there was a lot of it, he had also been told, it was a very valuable commodity. Sheriff Turner had been promised a share in what Milton was sure was going to make him one of the richest men in Arkansas. Being an opportunist, he would anyway have sold his services to the highest bidder, which in this case was not the county, it was Milton. He'd already stashed away a tidy little sum and was planning to live long enough to enjoy it on some little spread of his own down south where he'd come from. So he wasn't planning on taking any chances with John Thirsk. 'I'll need the best boys we've got,' he said to Milton.

'Take who you like. Take 'em all. Only get the job done,' Milton said in reply.

'There's something about that man I don't like,' Sheriff Turner remarked pensively. 'Men like him don't come along every day, and I've got a feeling

43

I've seen his face somewhere before.'

'I thought that,' added Johnstone. 'Frank Butler had a reputation for being some sort of law-enforcer down in Texas. He wouldn't talk about it himself, but word was he'd hunted down scores of outlaws and had retired here in Arkansas when he'd had enough and wanted to settle down somewhere with his wife and sons. And, of course, we all know how he met his untimely death.'

'If this man was to turn out to be a friend of his from the past it would explain everything,' Sheriff Turner added. 'It would also tell us what we're up against.'

'We are not outlaws,' snapped Milton, 'this is just a bit of sound, business-like consolidation. There is no future anywhere in these new territories for the smallholder and people like the Butlers either get big or get swallowed up. This ain't Missouri, this is Arkansas and we are not about to let the likes of any James Gang start springing up around here. I don't care what Frank Butler and his friends got up to in Texas, if this man Thirsk thinks he can set himself up here as some kind of Robin Hood he's sorely mistaken. Now you get out there and arrest him or kill him. And get it done quick, before others start thinking he might be a man to back.'

SIX

John Thirsk and Jesse Butler had ridden back to Horseshoe Farm. Jesse was struck by what John Thirsk had done, but it was not horror that he felt. Milton's man got what he'd deserved. But shouldn't it have been at the hands of the law? Except that he knew both the sheriff and the courts were in the pay of Milton. It gave him comfort somehow to know that at last there was a power in the world that would and could stand up to Milton. And it gave him even greater comfort to know it was a friend of his father's. He felt a lump in his throat at the thought of his father, and of how he'd been shot down in so cowardly a fashion. He knew his father had been as quick on the draw as John Thirsk, and that if Milton had tried to press his claim while he was alive it would have been a different story. Most likely their barn would have been standing now instead of lying in ashes, a smouldering wreck.

But beside the lump in his throat he felt a

growing excitement. This was not the end, it was the beginning. A war had started. Milton would assuredly see to that. When they got back to the farm he was, he knew, going to have to practise his shooting some.

'That was fast, John,' he said at last.

'Needed to be,' was John Thirsk's reply. He had been quietly pensive since they'd ridden away from Milton's spread. He'd killed a man without the authority of a marshal's badge to justify it. That was something he'd never done before and he wasn't sure why he'd done it now, except that he knew he'd stepped into a den of thieves. He'd seen right away the kind of man Milton was. He was no common criminal but was instead a man with an agenda and with money enough to make it happen. He had the powers that be in his pocket, that was obvious. Otherwise the Butlers would be safe on their farm while the wheels of the law, no matter how slowly, turned to find some sort of solution as to whose claim to the land was the right one.

But did this give him the right to act outside the law? He had killed Milton's foreman simply to send a message to Milton. For no other reason. But now that the deed was done somehow it was not resting lightly on his mind.

'What do you think's gonna happen now?' Jesse asked.

'That depends on Milton. If he's got any sense,

nothing. But men like him ain't usually got much sense. That's why they don't take no for an answer the first time.'

'Pa would have made sure he did,' Jesse said, 'and now we're gonna make sure he does.'

Jesse Butler was just a kid still, but one fast becoming a man. John Thirsk had, he reckoned, taught him an invaluable lesson. Once a man has indicated his thinking, act upon it. Don't wait to see if his threat's a genuine one. When you know what the answer to a question is likely to be, shoot first. Might's answer to the little man's defence is always the same. Do as I say or die. Suddenly he began to know why he'd done what he'd done back there on Milton's spread. He had no intention of dying. He hadn't survived a hundred dust-ups with out-of-control outlaws by thinking any other way. This was a free country all right, but only if you stole that freedom, just as Milton and his like stole, from decent, law-abiding citizens, their land and anything else of theirs they took a fancy to. And what made the difference now to his days in Texas was this: the outlaws hadn't just turned to dust and been blown away, they'd become politicians and now where there was bad in the land, they were it.

Jesse Butler and John Thirsk rode on in silence, each with his own thoughts, until they reached Horseshoe Farm. It was not dark, though dusk was falling. Johnny, Jim and the other men

were raking through the ashes of the barn, damp-
ening down any that were still smouldering. They
all looked up when they heard the two men come
riding in. Johnny went up to them.

'Sure am glad to see you two back safely,' he
declared.

'You can thank John for that,' Jesse said,
dismounting.

'Why? What happened?' Johnny asked.

'He shot O'Leary, Milton's foreman,' Jesse
announced.

'He shot O'Leary!'

On hearing it said, Jim and the others gathered
round. They all looked aghast. Just then, Mary
appeared at the door of the cabin.

'Ma!' Johnny shouted on seeing her. 'John shot
Milton's foreman.'

Gathering up her skirts, Mary came rushing to
join them.

'Is this true?' she asked on reaching them and
looking at John Thirsk, who had by now also
dismounted.

John Thirsk looked at Mary and nodded, and
then headed straight for a water-butt. It had been
a long, hard ride, without break, and he felt dusty
and parched. Mary looked first at her two boys
and then the hired hands. Any fear she felt she
concealed.

'Reckon you oughtta get back to work,' she said.
'It'll soon be dark, and we don't want any burning

ashes blowing up in the night and setting the house on fire.' They all looked at her, still too mindful of what they'd been told to simply take up again so easily the job in hand. 'Come on,' she said, 'Johnny, Jim. We can talk about this later.'

Jesse had followed John Thirsk to the water-butt, and the pair of them were refreshing themselves at it.

'Ma,' said Johnny, 'we gotta know what happened, so we know what's gonna happen next.'

'Later,' replied Ma. 'Leastways nothing's going to happen right now.'

Jim and the others returned to their work, muttering to themselves. Jim was the hired hand, their sort of foreman, the man they all counted on most. He began to put his back into his work again, as if nothing mattered more. The rest took his lead and followed suit. Johnny couldn't help but look over his shoulder to see what was happening next with Ma, Jesse and John Thirsk. He saw all three of them go into the house.

'Jim,' said Johnny, picking up a shovel and turning back to his work, 'what's gonna happen now?'

'The kind of things we're gonna need our rifles for, I suppose,' Jim replied in characteristically languid tones.

'That's what I was thinkin',' Johnny remarked.

In the house, Mary put on some coffee. She had already given consideration to the consequences of

John Thirsk riding out to Milton's spread that day. John Thirsk was his own man and if he wanted to risk his life on their behalf, well, that was up to him. He'd been a friend of Frank's, and no doubt Frank would have done the same for him. She knew a little of Frank's past, though he'd never really talked about it in detail. There had been money, and Frank had left them a fair bit when he died. She had given serious consideration to using that money to quit Horseshoe Farm and make a fresh start somewhere else. But she'd heard that all over the West small farmers were being threatened by big money and powerful men and she had decided that if they wanted to be farmers they might just as well stay put and fight it out here as anywhere. Besides, Frank had loved the place and had made great plans for the future. She wanted to fulfil those hopes and dreams as far as she could.

But there was Jesse and Johnny to consider. Johnny was still just a boy, but Jesse was almost a man. And so like Frank. Any move away from the farm would have to be with his consent. From what he'd said in the past, she didn't think he'd give it.

Taking the coffee from the stove to the table, she said to John Thirsk, 'Well, what happens now?'

'That depends on Milton,' was all John Thirsk said in reply.

'You killed a man, John,' Mary said. 'Don't that

also mean it depends on the sheriff?'

'It was self-defence, Ma, O'Leary was going for his guns,' Jesse said.

'I guessed it would be that. I don't see John shooting a man down in cold blood. But the sheriff is still gonna want to investigate the killing.'

'Don't worry about that,' John Thirsk said, taking a mug of coffee from Mary. He had taken off his Colt and was sitting at the table.

'We all know that the sheriff's Milton's man. He'll make whatever fuss over it Milton wants him to. No doubt he'll be paying me a visit here.'

'Then we'll be ready for him,' Jesse said. He hadn't taken off his gun and was still standing. He stood tall and looked determined.

'Perhaps I'll go into town,' John added. 'It'd be better for all concerned. Too many innocent people here could get hurt.'

Mary thought he was right, but knew she owed him something.

'John, you were on business for us when you shot O'Leary. We'll stand by you and take our chances,' said Mary.

'That's brave talk, Mary, and I appreciate it, but these men aren't particular about who gets caught in the crossfire. I'm here to stop any harm coming to you and yours. It's best I go into town,' John Thirsk insisted.

'Then I'm coming with ya,' Jesse said with determination.

John Thirsk said nothing. Mary too said nothing.

'I can look after myself, Ma,' Jesse continued, looking at his ma and knowing what must be going through her mind.

Mary hoped John Thirsk would say something to prohibit Jesse from going with him, but he still said nothing.

'And who's going to look after us?' she said at last.

'Jim can do that, and Jacob and Joshua. They've all got rifles and they can all shoot,' was Jesse's reply.

John Thirsk got up.

'Whether or not Jesse here comes with me is up to y'all to decide. No one's safe until this business is sorted out one way or another, and that's the truth of it,' he said. 'I'll be leaving in the morning – with or without you Jesse.'

'With me,' Jesse said emphatically, avoiding his mother's eyes.

'Well, I'll just go and unsaddle my horse,' John Thirsk said, putting his holster belt and gun back on.

Mary said nothing for a moment. She and John Thirsk looked at each other, knowing there wasn't in fact anything more to be said. As John Thirsk was walking through the door with Jesse set to follow him, Mary spoke. 'Just make sure then you leave a rifle and plenty of bullets for me. They burnt the barn. I ain't letting them burn the house down too.'

'But you ain't ever fired a rifle, Ma!' Jesse exclaimed.

'Maybe not, but there's enough daylight left for you to teach me how.'

John Thirsk looked at Mary and smiled. He thought of Rosalee, and reckoned she and Mary Butler were pretty much alike. He remembered once giving Rosalee lessons on how to fire the little derringer she kept concealed on her person in readiness for trouble in the hotel bar. After just one lesson Rosalee showed herself to be almost proficient in firing the gun. Here, now, Mary demonstrated the same skills with a Winchester. John Thirsk, the boys and Jim were all very impressed.

Night had fallen, and it was almost dark when they finished. Jim had unsaddled the horses and corralled them. It was obvious there was no other barn to sleep in, and John Thirsk looked about for somewhere else to bed down for the night. There were a few hours to go before he was ready to do so, but he eyed a small outhouse used for storing logs in the winter.

'I'll just get my saddle and bedroll and set 'em up for the night,' he said, walking in the direction of his saddle, hanging on the corral fence.

'You can sleep in the house, John, there's plenty of room,' Jesse said.

'You certainly shall,' said Mary, full of frontier hospitality.

'That's mighty kind of you all, but I'll be OK outside. I done it so many times it feels more natural than a bed somehow,' John Thirsk said, by now having reached his saddle and taken it in his arms.

'I insist, John,' Mary said, 'and I won't have it any other way. It might seem natural to you, but it ain't when there's a roof and clean, white-linen sheets calling.'

John Thirsk looked at Mary and the boys and smiled. There was a kind of sweetness to be had in being nice to one another when under siege from a world of baying coyotes. It was beholden of a man to keep his guard always posted, but he reckoned he ought to reciprocate in a way that allowed some normality to slip into things.

'All right,' he said, smiling. 'All right.'

The house wasn't big, but it was no mud dug-out either. It was only a single man's cabin when the Butlers first took it over, but they'd added to it, and Jesse and Johnny had their own bedrooms. Jesse gave up his to John Thirsk and doubled up with Johnny. Before retiring for the night both Jesse and John Thirsk took their Colts to pieces, cleaned and oiled them, and put them back together again. They both had Winchesters and did the same to them. Johnny watched for a while and then went and got his carbine, a Whitney-

Kennedy lever-action that his father had told him was his when he came of age, and followed suit. Mary had hoped that time was still some ways off, but accepted that circumstance didn't allow for it. Mary felt uneasy watching man and boy making sure of their instruments of death, but knew that in the West your best friend was your fire-arm and that you never knew when you were going to have to lean on it some. She was glad her familiarity with guns and rifles had now been extended somewhat.

John Thirsk and Jesse rode into Walnut Ridge around noon next day. They rode down Main Street with John Thirsk in his mind daring the sheriff or anyone to come out and challenge him. There were plenty of people going about their business, but none seemed to pay the two riders any particular attention.

Sheriff Turner was out of town. He'd left one of his deputies in charge. Deputy Board was sitting in his office when he saw John Thirsk and Jesse going riding by. The last thing they'd expected was for Thirsk to come into town. Deputy Board didn't know what to do about it. He'd been told they'd be going out to the Butlers' farm with a posse to arrest him. He knew where Sheriff Turner was, and he decided to go and get him.

Meanwhile, Thirsk and Jesse made their way to the town's hotel and booked into two rooms.

Anyone in town who was interested knew what Thirsk was there for, and the desk clerk was one of those that was interested. Word was out about Thirsk's shooting of Milton's foreman, and his reputation was growing accordingly. Mindful of this, the desk clerk was grovellingly courteous as he booked the two men in and showed them to their rooms. It made John Thirsk smile to himself. He was no stranger to hotels, and knew that the last thing any hotel wanted was trouble on the premises.

'If anyone comes looking for me, tell them I'm out,' he said to the desk clerk, flipping him a dollar coin. 'Then come and tell me.'

'Yes, sir, Mr Thirsk. Thank you,' the desk clerk said, in obsequious tones.

'The same goes for Mr Butler here,' John Thirsk added, indicating Jesse who was standing on the landing waiting to be shown to his room.

Neither John Thirsk nor Jesse had any more luggage than their saddle-bags, in which they had some washing gear. They weren't planning on staying for long and had only taken the rooms in the hotel as a base for their activities. Once Jesse had been shown his room and the clerk had left, he went to Thirsk's room and knocked on the door.

'It's me, Jesse,' he said, knowing Thirsk would be on his guard.

Thirsk invited him in.

'What do we do now?' Jesse asked on entering

the room and finding Thirsk surveying Main
Street from a window.

'We wait, Jesse. That's all. Just wait.'

'I'm kinda hungry, John. Is it all right to go and
eat?' Jesse asked.

'Maybe I'll come with you,' Thirsk replied.

Jesse looked at him and then asked, 'John,
what do you think's going to happen?'

It was obvious to Thirsk that Jesse was feeling
uneasy.

'I don't know, son,' he replied. He wanted to tell
him that it wasn't too late for him to back out, but
he also knew that it wasn't something Jesse
would do. Instead, he said, 'Look, Jesse, I've been
in many situations like this before. Milton
brought a war to you, now we've brought one to
him. He can either retreat or advance. But we
won't know what he's gonna do until he does it.
All we can do meanwhile is bide our time.
Something tells me the sheriff ain't in town. But
someone will have gone to fetch him. What's
gonna happen next will soon be apparent. Meanwhile, we eat.'

Jesse didn't look any the easier. He hadn't had
a chance yet to prove his mettle, especially to
himself. Thirsk put a hand on his shoulder and
with a reassuring smile directed him out of the
room, saying, 'Know where it's best to eat round
here?'

'Guess I do,' said Jesse, suddenly bucking up.

They ate in O'Mahone's Saloon, the place they'd gone into when Jesse first brought Thirsk into town. The atmosphere in the place tensed when they walked in and the bartender became uneasy. He remembered Thirsk and what he'd said he'd come to town to do. He took his and Jesse's order for lunch and waited to see what would happen. Nothing much did for an hour, and then just as Thirsk and Jesse were getting up to leave, Sheriff Turner and three deputies came through the bat-wing doors of the saloon and stood facing the two men.

'I'm arrestin' you,' Sheriff Turner informed Thirsk, 'for the murder of O'Leary.'

'Who are the witnesses?' Thirsk asked.

'Mr Milton and a dozen of his farm hands,' Turner replied.

'Did they tell you it was self-defence?' asked Thirsk, who in his own mind was getting ready for a shoot-out.

'No, they didn't. They said you drew first.'

'Did they now?' Thirsk remarked.

At these words the atmosphere in the saloon tensed some more. Men sitting at other tables and the bartender moved themselves out of the line of fire. 'I was there, Sheriff Turner, and I saw O'Leary go for his guns,' Jesse suddenly declared.

'You're under arrest, too, son, for being an accomplice. Now are you men coming quietly or am I going to have to take you?' Sheriff Turner

58

demanded. He wasn't feeling as brave as his words, and it showed in the way he looked. He knew that Thirsk was not going to do as he was bid, and he was just waiting for something to happen. The three deputies he'd brought with him were three of Milton's toughest men, but he knew none of them, himself included, was as fast as John Thirsk. He reminded himself that this wasn't the way it was supposed to be. That he'd rather have taken Thirsk at the Butlers' farm.

The stand-off continued for half a second more, until one of the deputies mistook a move Thirsk made to walk out of the saloon. His nerve broke and he began to go for his .45. In a flash, Thirsk had his Peacemaker out and the man fell dead. Then the rest of them went for their guns.

As the bartender dived for cover, Thirsk took Turner and one of the deputies, while Jesse shot the remaining one. The two men stood for a moment, their guns smoking. Jesse was aghast at what he'd just done. He'd shot and killed a man. It was in self-defence, which was OK, but nevertheless he'd just shot a man. He'd had the nerve to do it. He felt like jumping up in the air and hollering with delight. But he didn't. He knew it would not have been the manly thing to do. Instead he turned and looked at Thirsk.

'You did well, Jesse, real well,' Thirsk said, as he re-holstered his gun. Jesse did the same with his. 'Just like your Pa would have done.'

Both men smiled. Just at that moment there was a great thundering of horses' hooves outside. Thirsk went to a window to see what it was. It was Milton with about fifteen men.

'It's Milton, Jesse. Let's go out and greet him,' Thirsk said.

First though, he pulled out his gun and reloaded it, telling Jesse to do the same. Jesse was amazed at Thirsk's nerve. Was he invincible? Could he take on anyone? It seemed so.

They stepped out onto the plankwalk to find fifteen rifles trained on them. 'Try and draw now,' was all Milton said, sitting astride a palomino.

He saw the bodies lying on the saloon floor through the bat-wings as Thirsk and Jesse came out. It told him what had happened to Sheriff Turner and his three deputies.

'You're going to swing for sure now, Thirsk, both of you.'

'It was self-defence,' Jesse was quick to declare. 'Anyone in there will tell you that. One of the deputies went for his gun while John and Sheriff Turner were talking.'

'You can tell that to the judge,' Milton snarled. 'Now drop your guns.'

Thirsk weighed up the situation. Had he been on his own he'd have dived back into the saloon and tried to make an escape through the rear. But with Jesse at his side he couldn't risk it. Jesse wouldn't have known what his actions meant, and would have been cut down before he cottoned on. Had he not been Frank Butler's son, he'd have risked it. After all, it had always been each man for himself. But Jesse was too green and he hadn't come down here to get him killed. That wasn't part of the plan.

So, slowly. he pulled his Colt Peacemaker from its holster and threw it to the ground.

'But, Mr Milton—' Jesse began, only to be interrupted by Thirsk.

'Do as he says, Jesse. Just do as he says.'

SEVEN

Jesse Butler and John Thirsk, having given in to the inevitable, were taken into custody by the man Milton took it upon himself to appoint sheriff in the dead Sheriff Turner's place. They were going to be charged with murder. Milton's men had called for a lynching but Milton, feeling sure there was a watertight case against them, reckoned there was a lot to be gained by being seen by the townsfolk to be doing things by the book. Besides which, he didn't like dirtying his hands any more than he had to.

Word soon got to Horseshoe Farm of what had happened. Mary didn't know what to do, while Johnny was all for getting on a horse and riding into town there and then to bust Jesse and John Thirsk out of jail. Mary dampened his hotheadedness with appropriately restraining words. But someone else felt just as strongly as Johnny that neither man was any better than dead as long as

63

they were locked up in Walnut Ridge town jail. That was Jim.

'Johnny's right, ma'am. We gotta go into town and bust 'em out of that jailhouse somehow or other. Otherwise they's gonna die, as sure as butter is butter,' he said, with all the authority of a trusted hired hand.

'See, Ma, I done told you,' said Johnny, his reckless enthusiasm for the task rekindled by Jim's support of it.

'Yes, yes,' Mary said impatiently to him. Turning to Jim, however, she spoke with the respect due to a man who'd been her husband's oldest and most dependable hired hand as she asked, 'How are we going to do that?'

'I don't know, ma'am, but we sure gotta do it,' Jim insisted.

'I don't doubt that, but how?' Mary asked again.

They talked and talked, and eventually cooked up a plan between them. Mary, it was decided, was going to have to show herself at the town jail and make out she was the poor widow-woman going to console her elder son. They'd take the wagon into town. Jim and Jacob would accompany her and wait in the wagon ready, while she went into the sheriff's office to see Jesse and Thirsk. She'd take with her a basket of food for the two prisoners, only there'd be something more than just Ma's homemade apple-pie in it.

They decided the day was too advanced to do it

then. It would have to wait until the morning. Johnny clamoured to go with them.

'Johnny,' Mary said, 'there ain't no purpose to be had in all of us putting ourselves at risk. And besides, someone's gotta stay and keep a look-out here on the farm, otherwise we could find ourselves handing it to Milton on a plate.'

'But, Ma, I can shoot as good as Jesse and—' he remonstrated.

'I know, son,' said Mary, interrupting him, 'but we ain't all needed in town, and as I said, someone's got to stay and watch out for things here.'

Johnny wasn't persuaded, and kept on about it. At last Jim had had enough. He didn't normally come between his mistress and her sons, but he felt the occasion demanded it, not least of all because in this fight he, and not just he alone, but all the hired hands, were risking their necks as much as Mary was risking hers.

'You do as your ma tells you now, Master Johnny. This ain't a game we're a-playing here. It's a fight to the death.'

Johnny, recognising the authority of a man his father had always put in charge when occasion had called for it, took heed of the Negro as though it were indeed his father speaking and finally gave in.

'Thank you, Jim', Mary said to Jim appreciatively.

The next day, shortly after noon, Mary, Jim and

Jacob set out for Walnut Ridge. The two men were armed with their rifles, which they kept concealed under gunny sacks. Mary had hidden on her the Colt Frontier that her husband Frank had used, though unbeknown to her, all through his time hunting down and killing outlaws. It was loaded and ready-concealed in a bag in which she was supposedly carrying food for Jesse and John Thirsk.

They arrived in Walnut Ridge at around dusk, as they intended. Main Street was quiet. Pulling up outside the sheriff's office, Mary was relieved to see there was no one keeping guard outside. It told her that no one was expecting anyone to walk in and try and bust out John Thirsk and Jesse.

'Wait here and be ready. If there's any shooting, don't come running in. Wait till we come running out,' Mary said, as she prepared to get down from the wagon.

'You be careful, now, ma'am. And just holler if you need any help,' Jim said.

He didn't like the idea of a woman going in to do a man's job, but he knew Mary was nothing if not capable, and he had a lot of respect for her ability to make sure things happened the way she wanted them to.

'I don't aim to do it any other way,' Mary replied, looking at him gravely. Then, with Jim's assistance, she climbed down out of the wagon and steeled herself to walk into the sheriff's office.

She wondered which of Milton's hired guns had been appointed sheriff in the dead Sheriff Turner's place.

It was a man she didn't know. There were two men in the sheriff's office. One called Yardley, sporting a sheriff's badge, and the other called Milner, who was his deputy.

'Yes, ma'am, what can I do for you?' Yardley asked, getting up from behind a desk, as Mary entered.

'I'm Jesse Butler's mother. I've come to pay him a visit,' Mary replied.

There was only one cell, and it took up half the sheriff's office. John Thirsk and Jesse, who were lying on their beds, both sat up when they heard Mary's voice. All that separated them from her and the two men was a set of iron bars.

Yardley and Milner knew to be suspicious of anyone coming to see John Thirsk and Jesse.

'OK, you two. Just settle down,' Yardley said.

But Jesse wasn't going to be so easily told. 'Ma!' he exclaimed, more than pleased to see her.

While Thirsk knew it was best to just bide his time and get the feel of things before deciding what to do about his predicament, Jesse had been fretting about it. He was fearful of what was going to happen to his mother, Johnny and the farm.

Mary walked up to the bars of the cell and said hello to them both.

'Are you all right?' Jesse asked her.

Mary was about to answer when Yardley demanded to know what she had in the bag she was carrying.

'Just some food for John and Jesse,' she replied.

'Let me have a look,' Yardley said.

Mary knew it was now or never. She put her hand in the bag and pulled out her murdered husband's gun.

'Don't try anything,' she said in fierce tones, turning to face Yardley and his deputy. The two men were stunned into silence and inaction. 'I ain't afraid to use this,' Mary added. 'Now unlock the cell door.'

She threw down her bag and moved to a position in front of the two men. Neither had moved or said anything.

'Do what she says,' Thirsk ordered.

Collecting himself, Yardley spoke, 'Now, you ain't gonna use that thing, ma'am, are you?' he threatened.

'Ain't I?' Mary replied. 'Try me. Now unlock the door.'

'You heard the lady,' snapped Thirsk, 'and don't try anything.'

Yardley got the keys, which were lying on his desk, and moved slowly towards the cell door. Mary's eyes followed him. Milner stood watching, his right hand moving slowly towards his gun. As Yardley slipped a key into the cell door he went for it. Mary saw him and let go a shot. Deputy

Milner fell to the floor, fatally wounded. Yardley turned and went for his gun. Mary let him have it too.

Outside, Jim had heard the shots and was in an agony of indecision over whether or not to rush into the sheriff's office to see what was happening. He had taken his rifle from under the sack and was about to jump down from the wagon, when Thirsk, Mary and Jesse came hurrying out. They bundled into the wagon and were racing out of town as people were beginning to appear on the plankwalks to see what the sound of shooting was all about.

Jesse, hardly believing what had happened, was full of admiration for his mother. He suddenly let out a wild yelp and turned to her and exclaimed:

'Ma, you're a beaut, ain't she, John, a real beaut!'

'She sure is,' echoed Thirsk, 'she sure is.'

Mary was not so sure. She had killed two men, a sheriff and his deputy. Now she would be branded as much an outlaw as John Thirsk and Jesse. As they raced out of town, not sure where they were going, she couldn't help but wonder where it was all leading to. Some distance east of Walnut Ridge, they pulled up.

'Where we headin'?' Jesse asked.

'That's a good question,' Mary replied.

'Well, it don't look as if anyone's on our tail,' Jesse added.

'No, but there soon will be,' Thirsk said, looking hard into the darkness behind them.

There was a silence while they all contemplated the predicament they were in. The night sky was beginning to fill with stars. Fall was fast approaching, and it was going to be a cold night.

'We are going back to the farm,' Thirsk declared. 'And if Milton don't bring more of this war to us, we'll take it to him. We're not wild animals to be hunted down. You're farmers, and farmers you're gonna remain.'

'I think you're right, John. We can't suddenly go on the run. There ain't just the farm to think of, there's Johnny and the farm hands too. There's you, Jim, and you, Jacob, and your families. We've stayed put this long, we've got to see it through to the end, whatever shape that may take.'

'And we're with you all the way, ma'am,' Jim said. 'Ain't we, Jacob?'

'Sure is,' Jacob agreed, though wondering just how they were going to get out of the deep water they were in. He knew how mean white folks could get when fighting for what they wanted badly.

There wasn't a direct route to the farm and to avoid going back into town they had to cross a lot of difficult terrain. But, despite it being dark and despite some unnerving jolts and mishaps, they reached the farm by sun-up the next morning. The place was just beginning to come to life with the farm hands lighting open fires and brewing coffee. Johnny was asleep in the log house, but it was an uneasy sleep and he was soon woken by the arrival of the others. When told the story of how Mary had sprung Thirsk and Jesse from the town jail he was aghast. It made him disappointed to have to confirm that no one had come to the farm from town during the night. He was raring to play his part in resisting Milton and his men. After Jesse had cleaned up and whilst Mary was getting breakfast, he questioned Jesse in detail about what it was like to have killed a man.

'Well, it ain't that sweet,' was Jesse's reply, 'even to know that the man you killed was a bad 'un. All I know is I shot in self-defence, and I'm glad it's me that's alive and not him.'

'Where d'you get him?' Johnny asked.

Mary overheard.

'Johnny, do be quiet and stop trying to glorify something that ain't meant for it. Killing is killing. Jesse did what he had to, that's all.'

'Well, I hope I get a chance to show Milton and his gang a thing or two,' Johnny said, still incorrigibly enthused.

'I hope you don't,' Mary said.

Jesse said nothing. He was thinking about what was going to happen next. If Milton and his men came out to the farm, he knew there'd be a hell of a bust-up, and that most likely Johnny would get in plenty of shooting. But would any of

71

them survive it? He decided to go and speak to
Thirsk about it. Having told Johnny to stay put
and help Ma, Jesse went to find him. He found
Thirsk standing near the burned-out barn. He
was obviously deep in thought, and Jesse said
nothing to him for a moment. Then he asked,
'What are we going to do, John?'

Thirsk didn't answer for a moment. Turning on
his heels, he cast an eye over the fields. He didn't
see how they could defend it if Milton was to
descend upon them with an army of men.

'That's a good question,' he said at last. 'It all
depends on what Milton decides to do. But we
ain't got our horses and I don't suppose you've got
much ammo stored here.'

'We have, John. We've got a few thousand
rounds. That was Jim's idea when all this trouble
first started.'

'Well, that's something. But I don't know as we
oughtta wait for the fight to come here.'

'We've got enough guns to put up a good fight,'
Jesse said.

'Maybe, but for how long?'

'Do you think they'll be lookin' for Ma for
murder?'

'They will if it's left to Milton. No jury would
convict your ma or us, but I don't see Milton
letting things go to law. Whatever his reasons for
wanting this place, he ain't going to risk letting
the law decide things. He'll be coming to finish it

for himself this time. There ain't no doubt about that, son.'

'Why ain't he come yet?' Jesse asked, turning his gaze to look down the track that led to the farm.

'He wouldn't travel by night. But he'll be here. You can count on that.'

EIGHT

Milton was, in fact, in no mood to rush things. Killing was not really his forte, and it wasn't something he had had to resort to in the past. Before, intimidation and wrecking had worked. But his foreman, two of his appointed sheriffs and a handful of deputies had been killed. The last sheriff by a woman! What gross incompetence this had demonstrated.

He decided he'd have to try and buy off John Thirsk. Whatever it cost. Every man had his price: he decided John Thirsk would have his. He called for Johnstone.

'Johnstone,' he said, when his new foreman arrived, 'I want you to go and talk to John Thirsk. Tell him I want to talk.'

'Are you sure that's wise, Mr Milton? I mean, he don't strike me as the talking sort,' Johnstone said. 'And I don't think he's stupid enough to walk into any trap either.'

'He's killed men,' came Milton's harsh reply.

'Whatever side of the law he was on before, he's on the wrong side now. I am not exactly on that side yet. That must be concentrating his mind somewhat into wondering how he can get himself and the Butlers out of the trouble he's got them deep into.'

Johnstone was a simple man, if a bad one. Things were black and white to him. He looked at Milton, supposing that he, the one with all the money, all the power, must know what he was doing. Believing this, he did what he was told, got together as many men as he reckoned he needed to protect his own neck, and rode out to Horseshoe Farm.

Jesse Butler and John Thirsk were on the lookout for anything that might happen, and they saw Johnstone and his riders coming. Turning to Thirsk, Jesse asked, 'What now?'

'Get everyone under cover, Jesse. No one's to fire unless they fire first. Make sure they all understand that.'

The farm sprang into action and within minutes Mary and every last man of them were under cover, with rifles and six-guns at the ready. The riders slowed down as they neared the entrance to the farm and came to a halt just outside it. Johnstone guessed Thirsk would be waiting for him, and he called out to him that he had come only to talk and not to fight. Thirsk was in the cabin with Mary and her two sons, who were all standing by windows ready for any eventuality. The Butlers looked at Thirsk to see what his reaction would be. Opening the door by which he was standing a little, Thirsk called back to Johnstone, 'Say what you gotta say then.'

'Milton wants to talk, Thirsk. He wants you to come back to the Bar-X. He guarantees your safety,' Johnstone called back.

'It's a trap, John. Don't listen to them,' Jesse said.

'Tell Milton if he's got anything he wants to say to me or these good people, he can come here in person and say it.'

'Look,' shouted Johnstone, 'Milton's trying to be reasonable. He wants the killing to stop.'

'I think these good people have had enough of Milton's thinking,' Thirsk replied.

'It's not the Butlers he wants to talk to, Thirsk, it's you.'

'I ain't exactly in the mood myself to do any talking. Now you go back and tell Milton he can either let things carry on the way they are, or, if he's got anything new to say, then we're here to listen, if he cares to come and say it himself.'

Johnstone took the view that this was not the way people usually spoke to Mr Milton, but he was not blind to what he was up against with the likes of Thirsk. He'd been nervous about coming to the Butlers' farm to deliver Milton's message and he reckoned now there was nothing more to be gained from pursuing the matter further. He had come with six of their best men, but Thirsk had shown he could not have cared less, even if he'd come with sixty. Saying nothing but instead throwing a last long, penetrating look in the direction of where Thirsk's voice had come from, he turned his horse and spurred it into a trot, followed by the six riders.

'Well,' said Mary, seeing the riders disappear and breathing a sigh of relief, 'I thought we were in for more than that.'

'Yeah,' remarked Thirsk. 'Well it ain't over yet.'

'Do you think Milton really wants to talk, John?' Mary asked, dropping down into the nearest chair.

'Sure he does,' Thirsk replied. 'But only to try and buy me off.'

'And if he won't come here and you won't go there?' Jesse asked.

'Only Hell has the answer to that, son,' Thirsk replied. 'Only Hell.'

Later that evening after supper John Thirsk and Mary were alone.

'John, what is it about you?' Mary asked. 'Why are you risking your life by taking on the likes of Milton? Why are you doing it for us?'

Thirsk thought for a moment and then replied, 'How much about his past did Frank tell you, Mary?'

78

'Very little. There were rumours, but I never asked if they were true, until Frank was shot. Then it was too late. There was no one to give the answers.'

'Well, if he didn't see fit to tell you, I'd rather you didn't ask me.'

'Maybe I shouldn't but now I need to know. All I do know is that you and Frank were somehow good friends.'

Thirsk thought for a moment. Mary was clearing away the remains of dinner as she spoke. He watched her as she went about what she was doing. It made him think of Rosalee. She was a different sort of person altogether though. Rosalee was a woman of the night. Her whole life revolved around the hotel and the good times had there by one and all; Mary, he supposed, had never even stepped into such a place. He could see why Frank had married her. Could see why he'd want her to be the mother of his children.

'We hunted down thieving, murderous outlaws, Mary. Bank robbers. Train robbers. Men who took what they wanted from whoever had it.'

'So you killed people?' Mary asked. She had stopped what she was doing and turned to look at him.

'Yes, if there was no other way, and there mostly wasn't. And if we hadn't, they'd have continued on their killing sprees. Ruining the lives usually of countless ordinary people just going about their daily lives in the new towns and communities dotted about the Frontier. I was a marshal and Frank was one of my deputies. He was one of the best shots in Texas.'

'No wonder Frank kept it all a secret from me,' Mary sighed, sinking into a chair at the table opposite John Thirsk, 'though I don't know why exactly.'

'Would it have made any difference, if he had told you? Would you still have married him?'

'I'd have married him whatever. I loved him, he was a fine man. A good man, and a wonderful husband and father. But he could have told me.'

'Killing ain't to everyone's liking. And, besides, we got to thinking that maybe we were just pawns in a political game. You'd get to hear stories of how people had been run off their lands by the rich and powerful to build railroads and farming and mining empires. By people like Milton. Some of them became outlaws because there was nothing else for them to do. Often their families had all been killed by these rich and powerful men, and there was no redress for them. If these men didn't *own* the politicians who were supposed to be enforcing laws and policies to protect settlers on the homesteads they carved out of the wilderness, they *were* the politicians, and nothing much less than the barrel of a gun was gonna alter anything. Some of the people who were behind those barrels became the outlaws Frank and I hunted down.'

'Bad is bad and good turned bad is still bad. You did what had to be done, but you remained good men. The best. Frank was the best. That's why I loved him.'

'You must miss him,' Thirsk remarked.

Mary looked at him, her eyes filling. 'I do,' she replied. 'I always will.'

There were a few moments' silence while Mary collected herself. Thirsk felt deeply for her.

'What about you, John?' Mary asked, getting up and returning to putting away the dinner things. 'Is there no Mrs John Thirsk?'

He told her the story of Rosalee and the White Horse Hotel.

'She's a lucky woman, John,' Mary told him. 'I knew I was every time I looked into Frank's eyes.'

John Thirsk said nothing in reply. He feared that if he did, the passions that might arise in him would leave him with a greater battle to fight than the one already in hand. Instead, he said, 'Guess I'll go and see what the boys are up to.'

NINE

Milton's reaction to Thirsk's refusal to meet him was one of exasperation. The expected team of geologists had arrived. Their first impressions were that there was certainly bauxite in the ground, but how much needed to be ascertained by an extensive survey. This injected some urgency into the need to settle the matter with the Butlers. Strangers arriving in town were not something that went unnoticed and it was only a matter of time before the whole county would come to know what they were doing there.

Milton decided drastic action was called for. That fire would have to be fought with fire. John Thirsk was as good as a hired gun. None of Milton's men were up to taking him on equal terms. Like any professional he knew all the tricks, was ready for any eventuality. This meant there was only one answer. He'd have to hire someone to do his own dirty work, just as the Butlers had found someone to do theirs.

There was no sheriff in Walnut Ridge now. Since the last two had been killed, nobody wanted the job. No sheriff and no deputies. This hired gun, whoever he might be, could be appointed sheriff. He could then go about his business legitimately. Thirsk had murdered in Walnut Ridge and at the Bar-X. Most likely he had a price on his head elsewhere. His lawyer would be able to find out. In the meantime he'd send Johnstone to find the kind of man he needed to finish the job. The kind of man who could put both Thirsk and Mary Butler at the end of a rope.

Milton's lawyer made the telegraph wires hum but he could find nothing to damn John Thirsk. Quite the contrary. He found the man was a hero in the mould of men like Wyatt Earp. He'd been a marshal and hunted down men who were the Devil's own. He, Milton reflected quietly to himself, was a mere greenhorn compared to the least of the men Thirsk had sent to an early grave. He warned Milton of what he was up against. Milton took the view that it was now do or die, and he had no intention of doing the latter. Johnstone was due back imminently. Perhaps then things would begin to look a little less bleak.

It was another twenty-four hours before Johnstone did, in fact, return. He'd been to Paragould, a town a day's hard ride away, where a friend of his was sheriff. Sheriff Batchelor was as tough a man as you'd find anywhere, and he'd made Paragould one of the most peaceable towns in Arkansas. Johnstone told him nothing about Milton's war on the Butlers, only about the fact that a man had killed a sheriff and his deputies and that the woman he was now holed-up with had done the same in springing him from Walnut Ridge town jail. One other thing he did tell him, though, was that Milton was offering a reward to anyone who could bring John Thirsk in, dead or alive.

Sheriff Batchelor had thought for a moment and then offered to lend him one of his own deputies, a reformed gunslinger who'd drifted into town one day, met a girl and decided to stay. No one knew much about him and he was not, as far as he could find out, wanted anywhere. He was quick on the draw and anxious to establish himself as a lawman. His name was Pat Kinkaid.

'I'd like to meet him,' Johnstone told Sheriff Batchelor. 'But he is gonna have to be fast, if he doesn't want to end up just another dead deputy.'

'Well, I'll send for him,' Sheriff Batchelor said. 'Meantime, how about you and I go to the saloon and talk over old times and how I tamed this town? Come to think of it, Pete, how come you ain't done the same to Walnut Ridge?'

'Come on, Billy, you know I ain't the kind. I'd rather find a place out on the prairie to throw my bedroll down on, than have a place in town to hang my hat on. You know that.'

Sheriff Batchelor simply laughed and led Johnstone out of his office and down the plankwalk to the Silver Dollar Saloon. It was some time before Pat Kincaid showed up. By the time he did, both Sheriff Batchelor and Johnstone had eaten and drunk their full, and were demonstrating a great sense of *bonhomie*.

'Ah, Pat!' Sheriff Batchelor exclaimed on seeing Kincaid come through the bat-wing doors of the saloon. 'Come and meet my oldest friend in these here parts.'

'Howdy-do,' Kincaid said, taking off his hat and reaching out a hand to shake Johnstone's hand.

'Pat don't drink,' Batchelor remarked. 'Maybe's that's why he's so quick on the draw. So what are you gonna have, Pat? Your usual sarsaparilla?'

'Sure thing,' replied Kincaid, looking over in the direction of the bartender. Kincaid didn't like it when Sheriff Batchelor was on a spree, and was glad to see that this one hadn't yet gone too far. He didn't moralize about his drinking bouts, knowing he was a good sheriff and a hardworking one who never let the drink get in the way of the job a grateful town kept reappointing him to do.

'You sent for me, Sheriff. Any particular reason why?' he asked, pulling up a chair.

'Yeah, son,' Batchelor replied. 'I'm gonna have to lend you and your quick arm out to my old friend here. He's got a problem with a sheriff-killer over in Walnut Ridge, and no one fast enough to deal with him.'

'Sure thing,' Kincaid readily replied. He was enjoying being a lawman, and dreamed only of establishing a reputation for himself. 'Whatever I can do to help.'

Just as he had done with Sheriff Batchelor, Johnstone filled in Pat Kincaid about the problem with John Thirsk and Mary Butler, while leaving out most of the important details. It therefore seemed a straightforward-enough job to Pat Kincaid.'

'When do we leave?' he asked Johnstone.

'Just as soon as you're ready, boy,' Johnstone replied.

The next day they rode out of Paragould, heading for Milton's spread.

Kincaid had got his stuff together and said goodbye to his gal, and Johnstone slept off all the previous day's drinking.

TEN

Three days had passed, and no one had been near Horseshoe Farm. John Thirsk wondered why. He didn't think for one moment that Milton would come and see them himself, that he would be making a climb-down. If anything he reckoned he'd be regrouping and planning a more decisive approach of attack. He knew how these people worked. Theirs was a war of attrition, until in the end the little people were so worn down they simply rolled over and faded away.

'What's happening, John? Do you think Milton's decided to back off?' Jesse asked, finding Thirsk sitting with his back against a tree, stripping bark from a twig.

'I wouldn't think so,' he replied. 'Not with two sheriffs and a handful of deputies dead. What he started has got to be finished one way or another. That's the way it always is with men like him. I've come up against enough of them in my time.'

'So why hasn't he shown up here in the last few days?'

'He'll be planning his next move.'

'And what do you think that'll be?' Jesse asked.

'Well, that depends. I don't see him coming out here to settle matters face to face. Maybe he'll appoint a new sheriff and send him out here with a posse to arrest us. That's his only real way out of things now. Short of laying siege to the place and starving us out.'

'It seems an awful length to go to for a piece of land, don't it, John?' Jesse sighed.

'It sure do, son, but it obviously ain't as simple as that.'

As they were talking a buggy came into sight, heading for the farm.

'Who might that be?' John Thirsk asked.

'I don't know,' Jesse replied. 'I can only make out one person, the driver.'

'You'd better run and tell everyone to take up their positions. I'll talk to whoever it is.'

Just at that moment Mary appeared on the veranda of the house. She'd noticed the buggy coming up the track, and she looked over to Thirsk to see what he was going to do about it.

'Stay indoors, Ma,' Jesse called to her, 'until we know who it is. John's gonna talk to them.'

Throwing another look Thirsk's way, Mary turned and went back into the house. Getting her rifle, she took up her position by the window. John

Thirsk stood in front of the house waiting for the buggy and whoever was driving it to pull up. It was nobody he knew, but it was somebody who was well known to Mary and the others. Almost before Dr Nolan climbed down from the buggy Mary came out of the house and called a greeting to him.

'John,' she said, 'meet Dr Nolan. He's been a good friend to me and all the families moved on by Milton. Dr Nolan, John Thirsk.'

'How d'you do, Doctor, how d'you do? Pleased to meet you,' John Thirsk said, walking up to Dr Nolan and shaking him by the hand.

'I'm mighty pleased to meet you, too,' Dr Nolan said. 'The whole town is talking about you and how you've stood up to Milton.'

'Somebody has to,' Thirsk replied.

'Well, it sure is time somebody did.'

'Doctor,' said Mary, who was standing on the steps leading up to the house, 'won't you come in for something?'

'I don't mind if I do.'

Just then Jesse appeared. Johnny and the farmhands had all begun to show their faces. They were all armed.

'Looks like you're expecting trouble,' the doctor remarked as he climbed the steps to go into the house.

'Well, we didn't know who you were,' Mary explained. 'Milton's men were here two or three

91

days back, and we're expecting them to call again.'

'You know, Mary,' Dr Nolan said, 'we've all been worried about you since you sprung Jesse and John here. Opinions have been mixed. Some say you were brave, others say you were reckless, But the whole town is full of admiration for what you did, Mary, brave or reckless.'

'It was both, Doctor, but neither Jesse or I are complaining. And no one would have been killed if the sheriff and his deputy hadn't gone for their guns first.'

'Well, they weren't really a sheriff and his deputy, just Milton's hired guns hiding behind a lawman's badge.'

'That's what I figured,' said Mary.

She made a pot of coffee and she, Dr Nolan and John Thirsk sat down at the table.

'So why the visit, Doctor? You didn't come all the way out here just to check on our health, did you?' Mary asked.

'No, not exactly. There's a rumour going round town that I thought you oughtta hear.'

Mary and John Thirsk looked at each other.

'The word is,' the doctor continued, 'that Milton's found something in the ground and that this is why he's been driving people off the land. A team of geologists arrived a few days ago and they've been doing a lot of surveying work.'

'Is that so?' Mary asked.

'That figures,' Thirsk added. 'There's usually something behind the doings of men like Milton.'

'We noticed he ain't been working the farms he's driven people off,' Mary said.

'No one knows what it is yet, but it must be valuable. I just thought I ought to come out here and warn you.'

'That's mighty nice of you, Doctor Nolan, and I sure am grateful.'

'It means you've got to be even more careful. If he finds out you've got wind of something, he'll be even more determined to have your land.'

'Have they appointed a new sheriff?' John Thirsk asked.

'No, not yet. Nobody wants the job. Not while you're around, John. You've raised people's hopes and got them thinking that Milton can be stopped. Though if he finds what he's looking for and there's plenty of it who knows what lengths he'll go to get this place?'

'That's as maybe, Doctor, but it don't alter the fact that this ain't his place to have,' Thirsk said.

'Mary, have you heard anything from your lawyer yet?' Dr Nolan asked.

'No, but he said it could take months or even years to sort out.'

'And in the meantime?'

'He said to sit tight which is what we aim to do. Especially now we've got John to help us,' Mary replied, looking at Thirsk with a mixture of affection and gratitude. Thirsk returned her look with a smile.

'Well, your lawyer would know what your legal rights are, but Milton ain't shown much respect for them so far,' Dr Nolan said.

'Nor anybody's,' John Thirsk remarked, 'from what I can gather. But we'll be ready and waiting for him when he makes his next move.'

'You've handled him pretty well so far, and no doubt you'll continue to do so, but two sheriffs and a number of deputies have been killed. Someone's going to have to answer for that, and you can bet your life Milton ain't going to let it be him.'

So saying, Dr Nolan got up from the table, indicating that he was ready to leave.

'Won't you stay and have something to eat with us, Doctor?' Mary asked.

'No. I've gotta be getting back. That Annie White girl is long overdue with her baby and I gotta pay her a visit,' Dr Nolan replied.

'Well, thank you for coming out to the farm to see us, Doctor Nolan,' Mary said.

'That's all right, I just wanted to see you were OK and to tell you about the surveying that's going on. Can't think what Milton's found, but obviously it's something.'

Outside, Johnny and Jesse were standing by the doctor's buggy.

'Jesse, Johnny!' Dr Nolan exclaimed in avuncular tones on seeing them. 'How are you boys doing?'

'Fine, Dr Nolan, just fine!' the brothers said in unison.

'Glad to hear it, glad to hear it,' was Dr Nolan's reply.

They exchanged goodbyes with the doctor and Jesse held his horse while he climbed aboard his buggy.

'Y'all take care now,' Dr Nolan said, as he set off back to town.

They all stood and watched the buggy go. Then Jesse asked what the doctor had wanted.

'To see that we were OK and to tell us why Milton wants the farm,' Mary replied.

'Why Milton wants the farm?' Jesse questioned, looking first at Mary and then at Thirsk.

'Yes, Jesse. There was bound to be a reason. He's found something in the ground. Can't think what. There ain't never been no precious metals or the like round here.'

'Well, perhaps we'd better start looking, Ma,' Johnny remarked. 'Could be gold!' he added in clownish tones.

'Could be,' Mary replied, though with little conviction. Then she turned and looked at Thirsk. 'What now?' she asked.

'We wait,' Thirsk replied. 'We wait. It'll become clear soon enough.'

Mary stood and clasped her hands in front of her and let them rest on her white cotton apron, her back a rod of iron. She looked at her boys and

95

thought of her workers. More than ever she felt
Milton could go hang. She most certainly was not
going to.

'Soon be supper-time,' she said at last. 'Why
don't y'all wash up and come in?'

Jesse and Johnny hurried off in the direction of
the water-pump, leaving Thirsk and Mary alone.

'I'm worried, John,' Mary said.

'More worried than before?' Thirsk asked.

'Differently, I suppose. Before I thought maybe
Milton would tire and leave us alone. But now I
know he won't.'

'That changes nothing, Mary. Whatever his
reasons for wanting your land, he ain't gonna get
it. That ain't changed. I'm here to make sure of it.'

The look of reassurance he gave her buoyed her
up. Smiling gratefully, she turned and began to
walk back to the cabin to finish preparing supper.
Thirsk watched her, and then turned to look in
the direction of where Milton's men would come
from. That they would come, he now believed to be
certain.

ELEVEN

At the Bar-X Milton was being introduced to Pat Kincaid.

'I trust Johnstone has told you of our unfortunate predicament here and what you're up against,' Milton said.

'He has, sir.'

'This man's fast and he doesn't hesitate to kill.'

'I'm pretty fast myself,' Pat Kincaid replied, his right hand on his gun.

'Good,' remarked Milton, impressed with what he was seeing, ' 'cause you're gonna need to be.'

'I'm gonna need some help,' Kincaid announced.

'You can have all the help you want. Johnstone will see to that. You'll be handsomely rewarded and, of course, there's always the office of sheriff to be filled.'

Pat Kincaid was a man of declared ambition. In his youth he'd been on the wrong side of the law; now he wanted to be on the right. He grabbed his chance.

'A sheriff's badge sure would bestow more authority on a man than a deputy's from another county,' he said.

'That's as maybe,' Milton was quick to reply. 'But you've got a lot to prove yet, Kincaid.'

'I'd say I'd done that by being here. But I'd be a lot happier knowing I could not be gainsaid by anyone,' Kincaid replied, impressing Milton with his forthright tone.

Milton thought for a moment. He looked first at Johnstone and then at Kincaid. Then he looked through the window, which gave a panoramic view of his acres. Desperate straits call for desperate measures. And it would put Kincaid in his debt.

'All right then,' he said. 'Johnstone will take you into town and get you sworn in.'

'Thank you, sir,' Pat Kincaid said, his six-foot frame puffing out to its impressive bulk. 'You won't regret it.'

Milton simply looked at him. Regret? he thought. The regret might all be on your side, son, if you can't live up to your proud boast.

It took one visit to O'Mahone's Saloon for Sheriff Kincaid to begin to get the real picture. The bartender was no friend of Milton's. Tactfully, Kincaid told him the court would decide where the wrong-doing lay.

'Oh, they'll decide it all right,' the bartender

said, 'but it won't be in the way Milton wants. Especially when people find out what it is those surveyors are scraping around for. But before that can happen someone's got to arrest them Butlers and this here John Thirsk. So far that ain't proved very easy. At least not for a brace of Milton's sheriffs and their deputies.'

Slamming down his empty glass, Kincaid took his leave. As he walked down Main Street back to his office, he knew as he greeted people they'd be thinking the same thing as the bartender. That he was Milton's man. Well, he thought, his face red with anger and indignation, maybe Milton did hire him, but to be sheriff, not a hired gun. He was no one's man but his own. Milton would find this out.

TWELVE

That afternoon, Thirsk and Jesse saddled up two of the farm horses and rode them into town. They were not the best steeds in the world, but they would serve a purpose. Mary insisted to the moment of their departure that they were making a mistake but Thirsk had decided he'd spent too much time sitting around waiting for something to happen. A lot more of the old John Thirsk was beginning to surface as he fast began to appreciate the real deep water he was in. Milton was no better than the most base common outlaw he and Frank Butler had hunted down and killed in the name of the law. Milton may not have pulled the trigger but he called the shots, a crime just as heinous in any un-bought judge's eyes. Except that, in this county, any judge that presided over them would be bought. This fact alone made him decide that time had come to fight with the gloves off.

'Mary,' he said, as she made her last protest.

'The time has come to fight fire with fire and to take that fire right into the heart of their camp. We've been lucky so far. None of us have been killed or wounded. But that luck won't hold out for ever. Frank's already gone. How many more of your family do you want to lose before this thing is over?'

Mary said nothing in reply. She had followed John Thirsk as he went to saddle up. She knew life was cheap in the New World. Guns and disease took peoples' lives everywhere you looked. Disease was master of its own destiny. Perhaps the rule of the gun could be brought to book and tamed. If it could, she knew that only men like Frank and John Thirsk could achieve it.

'All right, John,' she said. 'I know I can't stop you. And I won't try and stop Jesse. But if you're gonna do it, do it right.'

Thirsk looked at her. She was, he had realized before, a strong woman. That she could be formidable he'd already seen. No one, he thought, was going to use and abuse her any more. It had to be them or Milton, if only to save Mary's neck.

'I will, Mary,' he said. 'For you, for Frank, for every single person who's ever fallen victim to men like Milton.'

Mary smiled and went with him to saddle his horse. Jim was standing by.

'Jim, you're in charge while I'm away,' John Thirsk said to him. 'Do whatever you have to to keep Mary and Johnny safe. And I mean anything. Keep a good watch out and if anyone comes looking threatening, fire first and ask questions later. Do you get that? Your lives and theirs could count on it.'

'Sure do, Mr John. I sure do,' Jim replied, fingering the rifle that had barely been out of his sight since the killing had begun.

'Good,' said Thirsk, mounting his horse. 'Come on, Jesse, let's ride,' he added, throwing a fatalistic farewell look Mary's way. She looked back at him, seeing Frank and feeling her heart fit to burst.

'What do you think we'll find in Walnut Ridge?' Jesse asked after they'd ridden a few miles.

'That depends,' replied John Thirsk. 'If they haven't got a sheriff, I don't think we'll find much.'

'But what about Milton's men?'

'We can handle them and they know it. I don't think we'll have much to worry about there.'

Jesse wasn't totally convinced, and his apprehension grew the closer they came to town. In Walnut Ridge Sheriff Pat Kincaid was still going about town, familiarizing himself with it and its inhabitants. He didn't find anyone prepared to condemn Thirsk or the Butlers.

The geologists didn't come into town. Rumour was rife. No one expected them to find precious stones or metals. None had ever been found in

Arkansas before, let alone Lawrence County, so
why should any now? But then what were they
looking for?

Pat Kincaid knew he would have to go out to
the Butlers' farm to arrest Mary and Jesse Butler
and John Thirsk. They had shot and killed
lawmen and would have to answer for it. Whether
they did so in self-defence against a murderous
Milton's corrupt ways, a judge and jury would
have to decide. But in the meantime they would
have to be arrested. That fact was inescapable.

He'd need help and would have preferred to
appoint deputies from the ranks of the townspeo-
ple, but he could not find anyone who was willing.
It would have to be Milton's men, or no deputies
at all. He had just stepped into his office, when
John Thirsk and Jesse rode on to Main Street.
Thirsk kept his eyes peeled but straight ahead of
him, while Jesse's darted all around, expecting to
see Milton's men at every turn. There were none
though. It was four o'clock in the afternoon and
the only people to be seen were townsfolk going
about their business. Some of them recognized
Jesse, guessing who the man with him was, and
tipped their hats in greeting to them both. They
knew there was a new sheriff in town, and
wondered if Jesse and Thirsk did. Somehow they
doubted it, the way the two men rode brazenly
down the middle of Main Street in broad daylight.

Thirsk pulled up his horse outside O'Mahone's

Saloon. Jesse followed suit. Dismounting and tying up their horses to the hitching-rail, they went in. As they came through the bat-wings, the place suddenly became quiet. Thirsk knew why and he didn't let it bother him. While Jesse's step faltered, his remained firm. At the bar he ordered a shot of red-eye for himself, and asked Jesse what he was drinking.

'Beer,' Jesse replied, coughing to clear a tightened throat. He cast an eye about the saloon and noticed that some of the men sitting at tables dotted about the place looked shifty enough to be Milton's men. It served only to make his unease grow.

'You back in town?' the bartender remarked, as he served Thirsk and Jesse their drinks.

'We sure is,' Thirsk replied. 'Looking for our horses. Any idea where they might be?'

For a moment the bartender looked taken aback. The presence of the two men in his bar promised trouble, and he wasn't quite sure how to react. Collecting himself at last, he replied, 'Perhaps you'd best ask the sheriff that.'

'Sheriff!' John Thirsk replied, taken aback. 'What sheriff?'

'The new one,' the bartender replied. 'Kincaid, I believe his name is. He's more'n likely in his office now.'

John Thirsk and Jesse looked at each other. The saloon was still quiet, as people held their breath, still waiting to see what was going to happen. John Thirsk took up his glass and knocked back the whisky in one go. His mind was working quickly, trying to decide what to do. Jesse didn't touch his beer. He wanted to keep his hands free for his gun in case it was needed.

'Give me another,' John Thirsk said to the bartender. Turning to Jesse, he added in gentle but firm tones, 'Drink your beer, son.'

Jesse did so, but with a hand that was not altogether steady.

'Kincaid?' John Thirsk asked. 'And who might this Mr Kincaid be?'

'I don't know,' the bartender replied, filling Thirsk's glass. 'He's a stranger in these parts. Came from Paragould, I heard said, to do the job no one in Walnut Ridge wanted.'

'Is that so?' John Thirsk remarked. 'And who sent for him? Milton, I suppose.'

The bartender made no reply, though his fearful look told all. John Thirsk knocked back his second whiskey and decided it was time to leave.

'Come on, son,' he said. 'Reckon it's time we found our horses.'

He pulled two dollar-pieces out of his waistcoat pocket, and dropped them on to the bar. Leaving, he cast an eye about the saloon, his gaze telling all if they tried anything, he'd be ready for them. Outside he stood on the plankwalk and looked up and down Main Street.

'Where're the livery stables in this town, son?'
he asked of Jesse.

'End of Main Street,' Jesse replied, pointing
left.

'Right, let's go and see if our mounts are there,'
Thirsk said, starting to walk in the direction
Jesse had pointed.

He strode out like a man who was master of all
he surveyed, rather than a fugitive. People they
passed on the plankwalk stood by to let them
through. Some doffed their hats, others simply got
out of their way. Their presence in town at all was
a clear indicator to those with eyes to see that
there was going to be trouble.

It wasn't long before Sheriff Kincaid was
informed of the two men's presence in town.
They'd hardly stepped out of O'Mahone's Saloon
when a little man, his gun and holster almost too
big for him, had gone running to tell the sheriff.

'Thirsk and the Butler boy are in town,' he
blurted out as he burst into Kincaid's office.

Kincaid was sitting at his desk going through
papers and Wanted notices. He looked up at the
busy little man who stood before him.

'All right, all right,' he said, 'calm down. Now
say again.'

'Thirsk and the Butler boy are in town,' spat
out the little man.

'Where d'you see them?' Sheriff Kincald asked.

'In O'Mahone's Saloon, but they've just gone up

Main Street. Thirsk said something about finding their horses.'

Sheriff Pat Kincaid still stood alone as the law in Walnut Ridge. No deputies had been appointed. He reflected momentarily on this fact.

'What are you gonna do?' the little man asked.

'My job,' was all Sheriff Kincaid said in reply. He stood up from his desk. 'Thank you for coming and telling me,' he said to the little man, pushing past him and stepping out of his office onto Main Street. The little man hurried past, heading for the saloon, there to tell everyone the sheriff was on his way. In the livery stable Thirsk and Jesse had found their horses.

'Hello, boy,' Thirsk crooned to his horse, patting its neck and blowing into its nostrils. 'How they been treating you?'

It was obvious the horse was very pleased to see its master. Jesse was too tense to wax quite as lyrical over his own fine breed.

'Where are our saddles and bits?' John Thirsk asked the liveryman.

'Well, they're over here, but you can't take those horses without first I get the OK from the sheriff,' the liveryman replied, somewhat fearfully.

'Go find him then,' Thirsk replied, 'and get it. But these are our horses and we're taking them. But before you go you can tell us exactly where our saddles are.'

The liveryman said nothing but instead walked

to where their saddles were.

Jesse grabbed Thirsk's and took it over to him.

'Thank you, Jesse,' John Thirsk said, taking it from him. Jesse smiled and went and got his own.

A few minutes later they were leading their mounts out of the livery stable into the failing light of dusk.

'What now?' Jesse asked.

'Well, I reckon we got what we came for. We might just as well head on home,' Thirsk replied in defiant tones.

Jesse felt somehow it wasn't going to be that easy. And he was right, for just as they led their horses onto Main Street in readiness to mount them they came face to face with Sheriff Pat Kincaid.

'You John Thirsk?' Sheriff Kincaid asked.

'And what if I am?'

'If you are, you're under arrest.'

So far Sheriff Kincaid's gun had remained in its holster. Thirsk at first just stood with his eyes fixed on those of Kincaid. He didn't know if he was alone or if there were deputies placed nearby to cut him and Jesse down with crossfire. The look in the sheriff's eyes however gave him the answer.

'For what?' Thirsk finally asked.

'For murder,' was Sheriff Kincaid's blunt reply.

'It was self-defence,' Jesse trotted out once again. His stomach was in his mouth and he was barely able to issue the words.

'That'll be for a judge and jury to decide.'

'Don't you mean Milton?' Thirsk suggested.

'I said a judge and jury,' Kincaid reiterated.

'Which I said was the same thing.'

Sheriff Kincaid knew John Thirsk was right. 'I heard ya,' he said. 'Come quietly and I promise you'll get a fair trial.'

Thirsk merely smiled cynically. 'Sheriff, I am riding out of this town and if you try and stop me, one of us is going to end up needing the services of an undertaker.'

Sheriff Pat Kincald pondered these words for a moment. He had heard the stories circulating about John Thirsk. About how fast he was with a gun. He knew they had to be true for him to still be alive.

'I am not Milton's man,' he said to him, 'if that's what you are thinking. If the Butlers' farm is rightfully theirs and they need the protection of the law to stop Milton taking it from them, they will, as long as I am sheriff of this town, get it. But you two are wanted for murder and I have got to take you in.'

Jesse looked at Thirsk, wanting to believe in what the sheriff was offering them but with no conviction it could possibly be relied upon.

'I know what your defence is. I've heard it said all over town. If it's true, you've got nothing to fear from a trial,' said Sheriff Kincaid, persevering.

'Except a bought judge and jury,' said John Thirsk.

Pat Kincaid knew Thirsk was right. But yet he could not let him and Jesse just walk away. His dilemma, however, was a short-lived one, for suddenly Milton, Johnstone and a dozen of Milton's men came riding into town. In an instant they were filling Main Street.

'Good work!' Milton exclaimed triumphantly over the din of horses' hooves beating in the dust.

It was his assumption that he'd come across Pat Kincaid making an arrest. He would soon see how wrong he was. He had hardly uttered the words of congratulation to Kincaid when the strawberry roan he was riding was shot from under him. In the commotion that followed Thirsk, his Peacemaker still smoking, mounted his own horse and high-tailed it out of town. Jesse was not long in taking his lead. Milton's men let go a storm of lead but too late and too wide of the mark to do any harm.

Milton managed to avoid falling under his horse but he was stunned by the unexpectedness of what had happened. Not even the thunder of gunfire was enough to snap him out of it.

Sheriff Pat Kincaid was also startled by what he had witnessed. His sympathies lay with the two runaways, but he had a sheriff's badge on his chest and he knew that what he was witnessing was a bad case of lawlessness. He didn't like it, but he liked even less the way Milton had come riding into town like he owned it. By now

Johnstone was beside Milton helping to steady him on his feet. The dozen riders were steadying their mounts.

'That son of a gun!' Milton spluttered. 'That son of a stinking, no-good gun!'

Suddenly he rounded on Kincaid.

'You gonna just stand there and let him get away with it?' he snarled indignantly.

'No I ain't,' Sheriff Kincaid replied. 'I'll round up a posse and hunt the pair of them down.'

'Round up a posse?' Milton near bellowed. 'You've got one here.'

'I'll find my own men for the job,' Sheriff Kincaid declared. 'It'd look mighty prejudiced if I was seen to be using yours.'

'Prejudiced? What the hell are you talking about? Haven't I just had my horse shot dead from under me? Whose side are you on, man?'

'The law's,' Sheriff Kincaid answered, his right hand poised and his eyes focused directly on Milton's.

'Now you listen here, and you listen good,' Milton said between gritted teeth, walking up to Kincaid to confront him face to face. 'Don't start playing any games with me. You were brought here for one reason and one reason only. To rid this town of a no-good, interlopin' murderer. Now if you aren't man enough for the job, say so. Otherwise take my men and bring in John Thirsk, Mary Butler and that delinquent son of hers before I get an army together and do the job myself. Am I understood?'

Sheriff Kincaid understood only too clearly. Except that he began to feel now he should take Thirsk and the Butlers in as much for their own protection as for the crimes they had committed.

'I will do my job, Mr Milton,' he said in business-like tones, turning and defiantly walking in the direction of his office.

THIRTEEN

A few miles out of town riding east, Thirsk reined in his horse and Jesse followed suit.

'It don't appear anybody's following us, Jesse,' Thirsk said, looking hard into the dark that was consuming all around them and listening carefully for the sound of beating hooves.

'Don't that seem odd to you?' Jesse asked, patting his horse's neck and calming it after its sudden long gallop. He thought of the farm horses they left behind, but supposed someone would take them in.

'It does and it doesn't,' John Thirsk replied. 'I think Sheriff Kincaid is a man of confused loyalties. Milton bought him, but maybe that wasn't how Kincaid had thought of it at the time.'

'So what do you think is gonna happen next?' Jesse asked.

'Not much at night,' John Thirsk replied. He thought for a moment and then continued, 'Jesse I want you to go home and make sure everything's all right there. I'm gonna find those geologists and get them to tell me exactly what it is they're looking for.'

'What if Milton raids the farm?' Jesse asked uneasily, apprehensive of being anywhere in the county without the benefit of the family's protector.

'Don't worry about that. My instincts tell me nothing's gonna happen to anyone out there while Kincaid is sheriff,' John Thirsk replied.

'I wish I could be so sure,' Jesse said.

'Look, son,' John Thirsk reassured him. 'He could have drawn on us back there in town any time he wanted but he didn't. We can trust him. And I've gotta find out exactly what is going on around here. I'll be back before you know it.'

'Why don't I stick with you tonight?' Jesse asked, trying not to sound scared.

'No, Jesse. Your ma will only get worried if we don't come home, and she may take it into her head to ride into town like she did last time. Besides, I reckon those geologists are hanging out at Milton's spread somewhere. It'll be safer for me to try and track 'em down on my own.'

Jesse was not persuaded John Thirsk was right, but bowed to his authority and did what he was told. He wanted to tell him to look after himself but got all choked up and couldn't get the words out. Instead he tightened the reins of his horse, spurred it and rode off at a trot into the

116

night. John Thirsk watched him go and then tightened his own horse's reins and took off in the direction of where he reckoned he remembered the Bar-X was.

Back in Walnut Ridge, Milton had told his men to pack it in for the night but to be ready to ride in the morning. He left them in town drinking, whoring and gambling while he and Johnstone rode back to the Bar-X. Sheriff Kincaid had decided he was going to ride out to the Butlers' farm first thing and do whatever had to be done to get the matter sorted.

As he rode through the night, Thirsk began to feel no compunction about killing Milton the next time he tried to get in his way. He wasn't afraid of taking on the whole lot of them, only concerned that doing so with Jesse in tow would get the boy killed. He remembered the many times he and Frank Butler had stood alone against guns as fast as any the West knew. He wished Frank were alive now. This trouble would then have been sorted a long time ago. He got to thinking about how Frank had died, and whether or not Milton had had a hand in it. He remembered a few of the other men who'd ridden with him and Frank. Perhaps he should have sent for some of them once it had become apparent what the Butlers' trouble was all about. He knew they'd have come simply out of loyalty to Frank. But where were they? Anywhere out West. Across the border. Dead even. He didn't know. And now anyway it was too late. Tomorrow, he felt sure, would bring a resolution to this conflict, one way or another.

The team of geologists was indeed housed in a bunk house. It was just gone nine, and they were all generally lounging about waiting for another hour or so to pass before turning in for the night. They started their work at the crack of dawn in order to cover as much ground as they could in the limited time Milton had told them they had to do their surveying work. They were greenhorns from the East, but were not unused to carrying out their kind of work in remote places.

John Thirsk looked down upon the Bar-X from, a wooded knoll. It all looked quiet enough. From what he could tell there were no look-outs posted. He decided to leave his horse tethered to a tree and to make his way on foot down to the bunk house. There was no moon and it was virtually pitch-black, but the ride through the night had given him enough night-vision to pick his way through the trees. The air was full of the night-time din of insects and an occasional owl hoot. The night air was cool, but not yet cold. Thirsk found the going easy, until he reached a boundary fence. He had no job getting over it but nearly ran into a ranch-hand who seemed to be making the rounds. After waiting a few seconds to make sure

the coast was quite clear, Thirsk made his way to
a bunk house. He crouched by a window and
looked in through a grimy pane of glass. It wasn't
the one that housed the geologists. He could tell
by the look of the cowboy types inside, about ten
of them, playing cards and swigging whiskey
straight from a bottle.

Outside the next bunk house were a couple of
wagons and in a corral nearby he could just make
out a half dozen or so mules. These he reckoned
must belong to the geologists. As he stealthily
sidled up to a window, he guessed he must have
found the right place. And indeed he had. Inside
there were half a dozen fairly sophisticated looking men dressed Yankee style. A couple of them
were at a table poring over maps and charts,
while another appeared to be going over figures in
a notebook and doing calculations. An older man
was lying out on his bunk smoking a pipe.

Thirsk had already decided his best strategy
for finding out information from them was to just
wander into the bunk house as if he had a right
to. He reckoned they were not to know who he
was. None of Milton's riders were in there as far
as he could see and so he'd be able to pass himself
off as an interested hired hand. Before stepping
out of the shadows he looked around to make sure
the man doing the rounds was not coming his way.
Seeing the coast was clear, he stepped up to the
bunk house door and without knocking let himself

in. Every man in the room turned to see who it was.

'Howdy folks! I hope y'all don't mind but I just thought I'd come in and talk to you about this geological surveying you been doing around here. It sure is something that fascinates me.'

'Come on in,' the man lying on his bunk smoking a pipe said, getting up and walking into the centre of the room where the table and chairs were. 'You obviously work for Mr Milton, though I don't recollect seeing you before.'

'Oh, there are so many of us and we ain't all here at once. This place spreads so far and wide it can take days to reach places we got a few days work in,' Thirsk replied, making himself sound as hickish as he could.

'This landholding is vast all right. I don't know how anyone can expect us to get around it and do our work in the time allotted,' the man with the pipe said, pointing out a chair to Thirsk and taking one himself.

'Well,' said John Thirsk, adding a 'thank you' for the chair and sitting on it, 'I've worked this place for years and I know there are parts I ain't seen yet. Besides which, Mr Milton seems to be adding to it near every day.'

'Well,' said one of the men who'd been poring over the maps, 'we've gotta somehow get a look over all of it.'

'Well, just what are you folks looking for?' John

Thirsk asked matter-of-factly. 'I ain't ever heard of there being diamonds or the like in these here parts. Nor anything else of any value for that matter. Except for cotton, and that we have to grow.'

'Bauxite,' answered the man, more a boy, being markedly a lot younger than the others.

'Bauxite?' questioned Thirsk. 'And what, might an ignorant fool like me ask, is that?'

'It's a mineral used for making the metal aluminum,' answered the boy with the notebook.

'No, I ain't ever heard of it,' John Thirsk said, scratching his head as if he were thinking hard.

'Well, you're gonna be hearing a lot about it from here on, because there is tons of it round here,' reiterated the young man who'd spoken earlier.

'Yes, well,' the older man said, remembering they'd been told to keep tight-lipped about their work at the Bar-X, and not sure just exactly to whom they were divulging all this information, 'there's still a lot of work to be done before we can ascertain that exactly, Charlie.'

John Thirsk realized he must not let his interest seem more than passingly curious. 'Well, whatever it is and however much of it you find, I sure do hope it makes Mr Milton's position in these parts stronger. He gives a lot of work to a lot of folks and people sure are grateful,' he said.

Nobody said anything, all of them thinking how

naive this stranger was. With their college and university education, they'd all come from big cities and were knowledgeable enough of the ways of the world to know already that philanthropy had not appeared to be Milton's strongest point. He was as slippery as any man on the make and to them it was obvious. Still, they were not here to put the world to rights and didn't bother to make the point to the hick seated amongst them. Only the older man spoke.

'Well, I'm glad about that. Can't be much to do around here, except farming,' he said, striking a match and puffing fast on his pipe to get a good smoke going.

'Mind if I make one?' John Thirsk asked, pulling his makings out of a pocket.

'Sure thing. Go ahead,' the man with the pipe said.

John Thirsk had began to think that he'd like to get a look at the maps on the table to see if Horseshoe Farm was to be seen on one of them.

'Are those maps you're looking at there?' he asked of the men at the map-table.

'Yes, they are,' answered one of them.

'I ain't ever seen a map of these parts. Mind if I take a look at yours?'

He was already on his feet and in an instant was standing over the table with the maps on it.

'No, not at all,' replied one of the men.

John Thirsk got him to point out where they

were on the map, where the town was and the country all around it. There were the names of numerous farms and amongst them was the Butlers'. Without specifically pointing it out, John Thirsk asked if this area was one in which they'd found the bauxite.

'Oh yeah,' replied one of the men, 'it's right smack in the middle of the richest deposits we've found so far.'

This was more information than the man with the pipe felt they ought to be divulging. 'Well now,' he got up and declared. 'I reckon it's time we were turning in. We've got a lot of work to do tomorrow and an early start to make.'

'Why, yes,' Thirsk said. 'I didn't mean to keep you, though it's been mighty fascinating. It sure is interesting to get a bird's-eye view of something I've only ever seen from the saddle.'

Thirsk extracted himself with his farewells and was soon stepping out of the bunk house into the night. It was much colder than it had been earlier on. Buttoning up his jacket and turning up the collar, he began to creep away. He'd gone only thirty or more paces when a voice called out for him to identify himself. He stopped and turned to look in the direction from where it had come. A man was standing less than ten yards away with a carbine at the ready. Thirsk reckoned to draw would only alert the whole farm to his presence. So instead to pretended to be one of their company.

'It's Tom, Tom O'Brian,' he replied noncha-
lantly, beginning to walk towards the man. The
name he thought as good as any.

'I ain't never heard of no Tom O'Brian,' the man
said. 'Stop and don't come no further,' he added
nervously.

John Thirsk didn't stop but kept on walking
towards the man, reckoning few people would fire
on an apparently friendly person in the dark just
because they didn't know who they were.

'I was just going to see how Mr Milton's
favourite mare is,' he said. 'She's about ready to
drop a foal and I don't want nothing going wrong.'

Before he'd finished saying it he was near
enough face to face with the watchman. The
watchman was only half taken in, but it didn't
matter. Before he could react John Thirsk grabbed
his carbine and struck him hard on the side of the
head with it. The man crumpled to the floor in an
unconscious heap. Taking a last look around to
make sure there was no one else about, John
Thirsk hurried back to where he'd left his horse.

FOURTEEN

Jesse arrived home very late to find his mother and Jim still up.

'What happened, Jesse? Where's John?' Mary asked anxiously on finding him alone.

Jesse told his mother the whole story. She was both appalled and given cause for hope. Like John Thirsk, she began to think that maybe there was benefit to be had from the appointment of Kincaid as sheriff.

'Ma'am, I fear we'd better prepare for the worst,' said Jim. 'Wherever Mr Thirsk might be at this moment he ain't gonna be much good to us if Milton were to send in his men now. We best get ourselves posted.'

'John said he didn't think Milton would do anything tonight,' Jesse remarked.

'Maybe not, but we best be prepared,' Jim replied. 'Dawn ain't very far off.'

Mary agreed and they set to work to make sure their arms were all in the right place and that

they were well supplied with ammunition.
Johnny and the rest, who were all abed, were left
to sleep, Mary figuring they couldn't do much
until they were needed. Jim decided he'd sit in an
old rocking-chair outside his hut and keep a look-
out.

'I'll sit with you,' Jesse said.

'You will not, son,' Mary said. 'You look
completely done in. There's some cold leftovers
from supper I could heat. You can have that and
turn in. We'll call if anyone we don't want to see
appears.'

Jesse, though, was having none of it.

'Ma, I ain't Johnny,' he said indignantly. 'And I
ain't going to no bed. Besides, I wouldn't sleep.'

Jim had moved off to his hut and was already
making himself comfortable in the rocking-chair.
It creaked as he rocked gently back and forth,
making a sound Jim's household would have
found comforting.

'You go and get that supper, Ma, and bring it to
me over at Jim's,' Jesse continued. 'And, Ma, don't
worry about John. I seen how good he is at
handling himself.'

Jim offered Jesse his chair but Jesse took no
notice and instead seated himself on a rickety old
table-chair. He felt a wave of sleepiness wash over
him as he took the weight off his feet, but fought
it.

'Your pa would be proud of you, son,' Jim

remarked, looking at the man who had so lately been no more than a boy.

'I hope so,' Jesse replied, 'I sure hope so, Jim. But he'd have been mighty thankful to you. I mean, you could have taken your family and left anytime and ducked right out of this quarrel.'

Jim thought for a moment. Despite being black, he'd never been treated as anything less than equal by the Butler family, a lead they all took from Frank Butler himself. Where else in the world might he have found that? Certainly he'd not found it between the end of the Civil War and the time before he came to work for Frank Butler.

'Jesse, your pa was good to me,' he solemnly said. 'He sure was a good man. He had a past and he talked to me about it once. He feared someone might shoot him in the back. It happened, he said, all the time to lawmen who had hunted down notorious outlaws. I told him then if anything was to happen to him, I'd stand by you all and see nothing bad happened. I meant it then and I ain't going back on my word now jus' 'cause that trouble has done come.'

His father's past had never been talked about before in front of Jesse. He'd been told that because he was his father's son, he'd be good with a gun, but no more than that. Now maybe here was someone who would tell him more.

'Jim, I don't know nothing about Pa's past. What can you tell me?' he asked.

127

'I don't know much either, son, except that he and Mr Thirsk were lawmen in Texas and that they'd played a part in bringing law 'n' order to that state. If your father lived to tell the tale, he must have been pretty tough and fast. Whoever killed him knew that, otherwise they wouldn't have shot him in the cowardly way they did.'

'Do you think Milton had anything to do with that?' Jesse asked.

'Everything that goes on in these parts is Milton's doing. But if he did, it don't matter none now, Jesse, 'cause Milton's got it coming to him no matter what. Mr Thirsk's patience done run out yesterday and he ain't gonna rest now till Milton dies. If Milton had anything to do with killing your pa, he'll be explaining that, along with all the other bad he's done, to his Maker pretty soon.'

'Whatever happens to Milton,' Jesse said, 'if he ordered someone to gun down Pa, I'll find out who it was and kill him, too.'

'Sure, son, I knows you'd do that,' Jim said in mollifying tones.

He could have talked pacifistic wisdom to the boy but he knew it was not what was called for just then. In America, where the proverb an eye-for-an-eye ruled, white folks seldom had the opportunity to turn the other cheek.

Just then Mary arrived with Jesse's food. The darkness was beginning to fade from the sky and dawn would soon be upon them. As she handed

Jesse a plate, she asked Jim if he wanted some coffee.

'Sure thing, Ma'am, but maybe it's time I woke Liza-Jane,' Jim replied. He held Mary in high esteem, and it didn't feel right letting her do woman's work without some help from his wife.

'Why, Jim?' Mary asked. 'The coffee's boiled and the mugs are ready. Why wake Liza-Jane when there ain't no need?'

Jim said nothing, but smiled.

'So, I'll get the coffee,' Mary said, looking into the quickening day, hoping she might see Thirsk come riding down the road to the farm.

John Thirsk was in fact still some distance away. He'd got clean away from the Bar-X and no one had given chase but he had got lost in terrain he barely knew. Realizing he'd not be able to find his way without at least some natural landmarks to guide him, he decided he might just as well bed down somewhere for what was left of the night and wait for dawn. When dawn came it still took him some time to re-orient himself He was hungry, too. He'd not been cold in the night, because there'd been a bedroll tied to his saddle, something he always made sure was there. But he was hungry. He looked around for something to shoot but realized there was not time for that. He had to get back to Horseshoe Farm in case

Milton's men, or even Sheriff Kincaid, showed up there.

After riding for some time through thick woodland he came upon a clearing in which there was a small cotton-grower's farm. He scouted about first. There didn't seem to be many people about and in fact the place seemed rather run down. But there was smoke coming from the chimney of the cabin. Deciding it would be safe to make a fairly open approach, he rode in through what was the gate of a fairly dilapidated boundary fence. He'd barely reached a hitching-post in front of the cabin when an old-timer appeared in the doorway sporting a shotgun which he was pointing in his direction.

'Stop there and identify yourself or I'll blow you head off,' the old timer snarled at him.

'OK, OK,' John Thirsk replied, raising his hands.

'Who sent yer?' the old-timer demanded, stepping out some.

Immediately the penny dropped and John Thirsk knew why the man was acting in so inhospitable a fashion for a southerner.

'Not Milton,' he answered, letting his hands drop a little.

'Keep 'em up!' the old-timer snarled again, then asked, 'How do I know that?'

' 'Cause I'm here in these parts keeping the Butlers over at Horseshoe Farm out of that man's clutches. Ain't you heard about it?' John Thirsk replied, knowing it would impress such a game old boy.

'I sure have,' the old-timer said, relaxing somewhat and lowering his shotgun. 'I wish we'd had someone like you about when my son and his wife and children were driven from this farm by that sonofabitch. Even though I shouldn't call him that, when I knew his pappy to be the fine man he was. Things around here was just fine and dandy till he passed on and that pup of his came back from the East. Anyway, look at me keeping you like this. Come on in. It is mighty early for anyone to be calling. You had some breakfast?'

'Nope,' Thirsk replied, 'I ain't had no chance to yet.'

'Well, come in. I was just about to finish cooking some. The name's Foster, Daniel Foster. I know what yours is. Reckon the whole county does.'

'Sounds mighty good to me,' Thirsk said, following the old-timer into his cabin.

Across a table, he told the story of what had brought him there.

'I sure admire the stand y'all are making. My son upped sticks and left when Milton fired our barn; and his men ran their horses through our cotton and threatened to come back and kill us all if we didn't accept his offer. But I told him I was not budging, whatever amount of money, small or large, and it weren't much in the end, I can tell

you, Milton forced on him for the place. I suppose
you could say I was a squatter now but as far as
I'm concerned what Milton paid for was the shit
in the bucket in the shed and not this farm.'

John Thirsk smiled at the way the man put it.
He looked about him at the cabin. It was as
unkempt as any place would be without a woman
and hired hands to do the chores.

'So where's the family now, Mr Foster?' he
asked.

'Somewhere's I don't know. I ain't heard nothing from them since they left a couple of months
ago,' the old-timer replied, looking sad and angry
all at once.

'Well, you show me how to get back to the
Butlers' place and I reckon it won't be long before
you can send someone to find your son and bring
him back.'

Daniel Foster looked at Thirsk across the table.
He knew a winner when he saw one and he reckoned he was looking at one now.

'I won't only show you the way, I'll come with
yer,' he suddenly declared, rising somewhat shak-
ily to his feet. It was obvious all the excitement of
Thirsk's arrival had taken its toll.

'Old-timer, if you were ten years younger, I'd
take yer,' smiled John Thirsk respectfully, studying Daniel Foster and reckoning he must be
eighty if a day.

'Less of the "old-timer",' Daniel Foster replied. 'I

may be old but I ain't run from any man yet and I don't aim to start doing so now.'

'Stayin' put here ain't running,' John Thirsk said. 'It's just that I gotta move fast to get to the Butlers before anyone else does.'

The old man didn't argue any with that. He knew he'd be more of a hindrance than a help to Thirsk, and let the matter go. His actions had shown his mettle and he'd made his point.

'Well, you settle things with that sonofaskunk once and for all,' he said, adding, 'Now finish that coffee and I'll point you in the right direction.'

Thirsk swung up on to his mount and listened carefully to the directions the old-timer gave him. Horseshoe Farm, he was told, was less than an hour's hard ride away. He'd be there before anyone could possibly make it there from Walnut Ridge or the Bar-X without leaving hours before sun-up, the old-timer informed him.

And indeed he would have been had he not got lost again. He rediscovered his way, but not before Johnstone and a dozen riders descended upon Horseshoe Farm, albeit to a cannonade of fire from the rifles of the ever vigilant Jesse, Johnny, Mary and Jim, there to lay siege.

FIFTEEN

Someone else who showed up at Horseshoe Farm not long after Milton's men was Sheriff Kincaid. While John Thirsk was biding his time under the cover of trees near where Johnstone and his twelve riders had taken up their positions, he saw Sheriff Kincaid ride fearlessly in amongst them.

'What do you men think you're doing?' Sheriff Kincaid demanded of Johnstone.

'It ain't none of your business, Kincaid, and if you know what's good for you, you'll turn around now and ride back to town,' Johnstone replied.

'What you're doing is against the law, which makes it my business,' Sheriff Kincaid replied.

Johnstone threw him a mean and determined look and said, 'I'm here to take in Thirsk and the Butlers, whatever it takes. Milton's the law around here and those are his orders.'

'And I'm telling you I'm the law. I was appointed Sheriff of Walnut Ridge,' Kincaid replied in equally terse tones. 'This badge is the

135

proof of it, and I'll shoot anyone here who tries to deny it.'

'Kincaid, I'm telling you one more time. This ain't your fight. Now if I was you, I'd get on back to Paragould where you belong, before something better'n worse happens to you here,' Johnstone said, looking the sheriff straight in the eye and pointing his Colt .45 at him in a threatening way.

John Thirsk watched the proceedings with a keen eye, his Winchester aimed at Johnstone's heart. One wrong move and he'd let him have it. While he was watching and waiting, Sheriff Kincaid was hatching a plan. He knew to take on Johnstone and his men there and then would be madness. Instead, he decided, he'd pretend to give in to him and seemingly to back off.

'I'll be back, Johnstone,' he said between gritted teeth. 'And if any harm comes to anyone at the Butlers' place, I'll hold you personally responsible.'

Johnstone looked at him and smirked. 'I don't think I need to worry too much about that,' he said.

'Don't count on it,' Sheriff Kincaid snapped back, before reining around his mount and riding back in the direction from which he had come. He'd barely ridden far enough to be safely out of sight when he was intercepted by Thirsk. He could hear gunfire had started up again behind him.

'Follow me,' Thirsk said to him.

'But I thought you were on the farm,' a startled Sheriff Kincaid replied.

'Well, as you can see, I'm not,' Thirsk replied. 'Come on, follow me, and we'll give Johnstone and his gang a little of what they've got coming to them.'

Smiling, Sheriff Kincaid spurred his horse into a trot to follow Thirsk into the trees. Neither Johnstone, nor any of his men, noticed the two men take up positions behind evergreens less than fifty yards behind them. With his first shot Thirsk winged Johnstone, who turned in stunned surprise to see where the shot had come from. But before he could react any further a second bullet from Thirsk's Winchester sunk deep into his heart, killing him instantly. Kincaid was at first taken aback by Thirsk's ruthless slaying of Johnstone, but in an instant realized it was the only way. As the dead Johnstone's men began to return fire, he let rip with his own weapon and three of them fell to the ground, fatally wounded. The rest began to back off in the direction of their tethered horses.

'Let them go,' John Thirsk said, ceasing firing. 'Let them go.'

He was reckoning that the sooner they high-tailed it out of there, the sooner he and Kincaid could ride into Horseshoe Farm to see what damage had been done there. They found, fortunately, that no one had been hurt. Only windows shattered and wood peppered and splintered. The relief felt by Mary Butler at the sight of Thirsk riding into their midst was unbounded. As the tension broke, Johnny, whose adrenaline was still flowing, began to congratulate himself with whoops and hollers at surviving his first gunfight. Jim and Jesse simply looked at each other and smiled with relief. They all gathered around Thirsk and Kincaid as the two men dismounted their horses. Glad in the knowledge they had all survived, they began to find out from one another just how. Sheriff Kincald was not part of this comradely grouping and he sensed it. While they talked to one another, he slipped quietly into the background and walked over to where work had been going on to rebuild the burned-out barn.

His mind went to the job he had set out from Walnut Ridge to do. That had all changed now, he knew. Once Milton heard what had happened to Johnstone and the others they had killed, he would he knew be gunning for him as well as Thirsk and the Butlers. He guessed now that something definite had to be done. So his thoughts were running when Mary and Thirsk approached him.

'Sheriff, John has told me what you did and I want to thank you for it. You probably saved our lives,' Mary said.

138

'It's not me, it's John you've got to thank,' Sheriff Kincaid replied modestly.

'Well, both of you,' Mary said, looking from one to the other.

'What happened back there has changed everything,' Kincaid remarked. 'What Milton had sent his men to do was illegal but he won't care about that, and when he finds out what's happened to Johnstone and his men he'll be pretty mad. I don't think we can wait to see what he does next. We gotta go for him. Which means he's gotta be arrested, and since I'm the law around here, I gotta do it.'

Thirsk looked at Kincaid and thought for a moment. Arresting Milton was not going to be easy.

'I was telling Mary and the boys that I found out what it is Milton is surveying for round here. It's a stuff called bauxite, there's plenty of it and it'll fetch a fortune. Horseshoe Farm is right smack in the middle of the richest deposits.'

'There had to be something more than land and cotton behind all this trouble,' remarked Kincaid.

'Yes,' agreed Mary, 'and a lot of people are going to be very unhappy about it once news of what it's all been about begins to spread.'

'Sheriff, I think we need to go into town and get Mary's lawyer to serve some kind of injunction on Milton to get all this nonsense stopped,' Thirsk said. 'We can keep on shooting it out amongst

ourselves, but it doesn't get Mary's problems any
nearer being solved.'

'You're right, John. And besides, we gotta get
these charges of murder against y'all dropped
before Milton can get on to his powerful friends
and frustrate whatever chances we've got of nail-
ing him and clearing your names. Now, Mary, who
is your lawyer?'

'There's only one in town, Solomon Mayer, but
he don't seem to hold no truck with Milton. He
don't seem to be in town much, though, but he's
been investigating our title and is trying to get it
established,' Mary replied.

'Right, John, you and I had better go into town
and hope he's there,' Kincaid said.

'And what about us?' Mary asked.

'You'd better come, too,' Thirsk replied before
Kincaid had a chance to. 'All of you. Hired hands
and all. There's no telling how Milton'll react
when he finds out what's happened.'

'Travel light,' Kincaid. 'You should be back here
in a few days. Either Milton will be behind bars or
you'll be on your way back here with the army to
protect you.'

Thirsk couldn't help but feel Kincaid was talking a mite optimistic. Men like Milton were not
easy to shift, but he hoped Solomon Mayer would
be in town and that something could be achieved.

They arrived in Walnut Ridge a couple of hours
before sundown and put up in the hotel. As luck

would have it, Solomon Mayer had come in on the morning stage. The town was buzzing with what had happened out at Horseshoe Farm. On seeing them all come riding down Main Street the citizens of the town seemed to let out a collective gasp. As dusk began to fall the streets cleared and everyone kept out of sight and harm's way.

Leaving the Butlers in the protection of Thirsk, Kincaid went to bring Solomon Mayer to the hotel. He found him in his office.

'Town's got a new sheriff, then,' Mayer remarked to Kincaid by way of a greeting. 'I been hearing you ain't exactly been dancing to Milton's tune though.'

Mayer was a tall, portly man with a thin head of greying, wiry hair.

'I don't dance to any tune but that of the law. I warned Milton of this fact but he didn't seem to see it mattered,' Kincaid replied. 'We're gonna have to show him it does.'

'Brave words,' Mayer answered. 'What you got in mind apart from more of this war that's been raging?'

'Mary Butler's under my protection in Adam's Hotel. She's asked me to ask you to come over there with me and see her.'

'Right,' Mayer replied, 'let's get over there then. I could do with a spot of something to eat. We can talk over dinner.'

Kincaid smiled to himself, admiring of Mayer's

urbane manner. He couldn't help but feel, however, it would be more suited to a town in the East than to one establishing itself on the new frontier. For this reason he was glad he had a man like Thirsk on his side.

Once arrived at the hotel, they soon found Mary Butler.

'Mrs Butler, my good lady, I am glad to find you safe and I trust well,' Mayer said to her by way of greeting.

'Thank you, Mr Mayer,' was Mary's reply. 'But only thanks to Sheriff Kincaid here and John Thirsk. Even now John is making sure me and my family and workers stay that way.'

Mayer sought an explanation of what Mary had said, and was given a detailed account of the events of the last few days. As he listened his stomach rumbled, but an opportunity to repair to the hotel's dining-room for dinner did not present itself – at first, anyway.

Solomon Mayer frowned at everything he heard. When Mary had finished he thought for a moment, and then remarked, 'I fancied the time would come when someone would make a stand against Milton's heavy-armed tactics. Except that now you stand accused of murder. Sheriff,' he said, turning to Kincaid, 'it seems to me the next move is up to you. What are your intentions with regard to all this?'

'My priority at the moment is to stop Milton

and bring him to book,' replied Kincaid.

'Which action in a court of law would put all the guilt firmly at Milton's feet, by virtue of which fact my client would be found innocent of all charges levied against her on the grounds of self-defence,' Solomon Mayer neatly concluded.

'That's how I see it,' Kincaid agreed.

'And the same would apply to my son and John,' Mary added.

'Precisely so,' Mayer remarked, adding, 'and what you want from me, I take it, is a warrant for Milton's arrest.'

'That is it precisely,' Kincaid concluded.

'Well, it will need the signature of a judge,' said Mayer, who felt deeper rumblings in his stomach than before. 'But perhaps that is something we could discuss over dinner.'

Mary, who was used to Mayer's deliberating ways, found herself as always instilled with confidence by his methodical approach to solving her problems.

'Yes,' she agreed. 'We can only hope Milton will allow us the luxury of finishing it undisturbed.'

Kincaid was asked to join them, which he agreed to do, though somewhat unsurely. Mary did not feel dressed for the occasion but felt under the circumstances allowances could be made for so unfortunate a fact.

No such niceties were being engaged in at the

Bar-X, where Milton was instead busily deciding his next move. Johnstone had been the man to replace O'Leary, but there was no one of a calibre to replace Johnstone. Who now, he had been asking himself, could he appoint to settle this thing once and for all with Thirsk and the yellow-bellied turncoat Kincaid? There was no one, yet he was averse to doing the dirty work himself. But he had, he decided, no choice. In the morning he would pay the Butlers and their knight in shining armour a visit. He would go with as many men as he could muster, and he would go in with guns blazing.

While Solomon Mayer, Mary Butler and Sheriff Kincaid were dining, John Thirsk and Jesse were scouting about town. There were a few rough-necks painting the town red, but none that looked like they were Milton's men.

'It seems,' Jesse remarked, 'that they've learned what's good for them, and are staying away.'

This was naive, but Thirsk decided he would not embarrass Jesse by telling him so. Instead, he said, 'Could be, but more likely they're all back at the Bar-X while Milton decides what to do next. He may know we're in town, he may not. If he doesn't, he'll know before much longer.'

They were walking along the plankwalk, and as Thirsk spoke they came up level with O'Mahone's Saloon.

'It's gonna be a long night, Jess. How's about we have something to bolster us up?' Thirsk asked.

'Sure thing,' Jesse replied.

They found a lively night going on in the saloon. They'd been there earlier but it had been quiet then. Now there were a lot more people. A piano-player tinkled vaudeville songs and good-time girls kept men happy. Thirsk and Jesse thought they recognized some of the new faces, but were not unduly concerned by the fact. All seemed to be having far too good a time to pay them much heed.

'What're you drinking, Jesse?' Thirsk asked, as they approached the bar.

'Beer, I guess,' was Jesse's reply.

John Thirsk ordered his usual red-eye. He was about to raise a jolt-glass to his lips, when a voice boomed out, 'John Thirsk! Butcher of men from the state of Texas!'

Thirsk froze momentarily. Then, collecting himself, he knocked back the glass's contents, put it down in front of him and turned to face the one desperado who had crossed his path but who through a lucky break had got away to live another day.

'Johnny Red,' he said, recognizing the man instantly, 'I'd'a thought you'd have been holed up somewhere in Mexico by now.'

'I was, except I got a little homesick. I hadn't expected to bump into your old partner Frank

Butler, though, Then I heard you was in these parts. I don't see no badge, Marshal. Does that mean you've turned as bad as rumour has it you have?'

Jesse's interest in the stranger suddenly took on a different dimension when he heard his father's name mentioned. Thirsk could sense it.

'Leave this to me, Jesse,' he said.

As he spoke, the area around him and Johnny Red began to clear. Jesse, though, didn't move. 'You killed Pa?' he suddenly let out in tones that were a mixture of hurt and growing anger.

'Jesse, I said leave it to me,' Thirsk repeated.

But Jesse was not listening. He was enough his father's son and had spent enough learning time in the company of Thirsk to not not do what he felt compelled to do next. His draw was fast but not yet fast enough to outdraw the likes of Johnny Red. Thirsk's was, though. Frank Butler's murderer was dead before he had the chance to detonate the bullet that would have slammed murderously into Jesse Butler's chest.

The whole saloon looked on, stunned. Thirsk merely stepped over to where the outlaw had fallen and prodded him with a foot. He knew he'd be dead but took the precaution, as he always did, of making sure.

'Reckon,' he said, 'we'd better go and tell Kincaid there's work here for the undertaker to do.'

146

Jesse had been stunned into silence. He knew it could have been him lying there dead instead of Johnny Red.

'Come on, son,' Thirsk said to him, re-holstering his gun.

Jesse followed. He could find no words to speak. But inside he began to feel grow a satisfying feeling that he'd played his part in avenging the murder of his father.

SIXTEEN

Adam's Hotel was almost opposite O'Mahone's Saloon. Sheriff Kincaid, Mary Butler and Solomon Mayer were finishing their after-dinner coffee when they heard gun shots. Their thoughts immediately turned to Milton. Was he in town?

'Trouble?' Mary queried.

'I'll find out,' said Kincaid, jumping to his feet.

He rushed out of the hotel, but had barely stepped on to Main Street when he came upon Thirsk and Jesse coming to find him.

'What was it?' he asked, looking up and down Main Street, half expecting to see men and horses.

'Someone claiming to have killed Jesse's father,' replied Thirsk. 'Thought he'd have a poke at me.'

'Where is he now?' Kincaid asked.

'In Hell, regrettin' it,' Thirsk said. Turning to Jesse, he added, 'Jesse, go tell your mother.' Looking back at Kincaid, he said, 'Sheriff, we best go to your office.'

Jesse, throwing a nod Thirsk's way, did as was suggested. Thirsk watched him go, and then followed Kincaid to his office. They'd only gone a few yards when the little man, who earlier had taken it upon himself to be the new sheriff's informer, came rushing up to them.

'Thirsk here shot in self-defence, Sheriff. Saw it with my own eyes,' he blurted out, full of the busybody's uncontainable excitement.

'Best you or someone find the corpse an undertaker,' Kincaid said, hardly pausing to look at him.

'Sure thing, Sheriff,' the little man said. 'See to it now myself.'

And with that, he hurried off into the night.

'How d'you get on with the lawyer?' Thirsk asked Kincaid, as they strode into his office.

'Well, he's with us but says you can get issued as many injunctions as you like but when it comes to enforcing them it's a different matter. Milton's the power in these parts, and that's about it. I've got plenty of grounds for arresting him but it ain't gonna be any easier than getting out an injunction to keep him from molesting the Butler family. He owns everyone and everything around here, and that includes the judges.'

Thirsk thought for a moment. By the time they were seated the idea Thirsk had been kicking around in his head was ready to be voiced.

'Well, guess we'll have to do it without a warrant, won't we?' he said.

'We?' questioned Kincaid.

'Yes, we. Make me a deputy, Sheriff.'

Kincaid studied Thirsk for a moment. He hardly knew the man, except by the things he'd achieved in making a stand against Milton. Johnstone had given him to believe that he was an outlaw with a price on his head, but he had looked through all the Wanted notices there were in the office and had not come up with anything with Thirsk's name or face on it. He decided he'd have to ask him outright.

'I need to know about you, John, if I'm to give you a badge. Johnstone said you were a man wanted clean across Texas and Oklahoma. A murderer. Is it true?'

'He would say that, wouldn't he?' Thirsk replied, smiling. But then, suddenly, a grave look furrowed his brow and filled his eyes with serious intent. 'Sheriff,' he said. 'I'm gonna get Milton with or without a badge. It'd be better if it was with a badge, but, either way, it's gonna happen.'

'Look, John, I just need to know. I want to do this thing right, otherwise Milton's gonna get away with it. The lawyers he'll be able to hire will run rings around the State's,' Kincaid said.

'All right, Kincaid. I don't know as you'll believe what I'm gonna tell you,' Thirsk replied, 'but I'll tell it to you anyway.'

He told Kincaid everything about himself and about his partnership with Frank Butler. The

151

sheriff listened, hardly able to credit what he was
hearing. He guessed it must all be true. Thirsk he
knew, was not the sort of man who had to invent
a past. His achievements since arriving in Walnut
Ridge were enough to give the truth to any
fantastic tales he might be telling.

'There's you, a marshal, and here's me getting
ready to pin a deputy's badge on you,' Kincaid
remarked, his voice full of incredulity and not a
little awe.

'Was a marshal,' John Thirsk corrected him. 'I
don't aim to get back into being a lawman, just to
put a stop to a greedy landowner and his grabbing
ways. I had a gutful of corruption in Texas and I
knew there was no beating it, not without as
much money as the fat-cats and politicians there
had. But here it's different. It's Frank's widow and
that makes it personal.'

'OK,' said Kincaid. 'However many of Milton's
men you've killed, I don't think the folk of this
town will hold it against you, or me, for pinning a
badge on your chest.'

He suddenly felt all of his young years. He'd
told Thirsk nothing about his outlaw past, but
didn't reckon he had to. He'd killed no one and,
compared to the men Thirsk had hunted down, he
had just been a kid playing at it. Besides, he was
sheriff now and it was important for him to be
seen to have changed and be capable of doing a
job that proved it. Added to which, it was a job he

aimed to keep. Back in Paragould he'd have to wait for Sheriff Batchelor to bite the dust or retire before he could step into his shoes, and that could take a long time. Too long maybe, when he had a gal he aimed to marry and start a family with.

'When shall we do it?' he asked Thirsk.

'Well, it's too late tonight. First thing tomorrow,' Thirsk replied. He wasn't a religious man but if he'd learned one thing in life, it was that even though the devil took care of his own, it was never well enough. Time always told in God's favour. 'We'll take him before breakfast.'

'That's if he don't show up here first,' Kincaid remarked.

'I don't think he'll do that. He'll know by now what happened out at Horseshoe Farm and he'll be busy regrouping his forces. I don't know how many men he's got working for him, nor how many of them gun-tote for him, but he threatened us with an army. Reckon he knows by now he'd better not show up again with anything less. Meanwhile, Sheriff, ain't there something you've gotta give me?'

Sheriff Kincaid couldn't figure what he meant. He looked at John Thirsk quizzically.

'Well, you are the sheriff, ain't you?' John Thirsk remarked, with a sardonic smile. 'Am I your deputy or not?'

It was late by the time Thirsk returned to Adam's

153

Hotel. Mary had gone to her room. He could imagine what must have been going through her mind, and decided he'd go and see her. He didn't know where Jesse was but hoped he too was in his room. Sheriff Kincaid had said he'd keep watch through the night. Thirsk had laughed, telling him he reckoned he didn't need to. The little man would soon come running to tell him if Milton or any of his men showed up anywhere near town.

Going upstairs, he went to Mary's room and knocked quietly on the door.

'Mary, it's me, John,' he whispered.

When he got no reply he turned the handle of the door and crept quietly in. Mary's lamp was burning but she was lying back against her pillows asleep, a small lace handkerchief in her hand. He crept up to her but she didn't wake until she felt the tender touch of his hand upon hers. Her need for him to comfort her was great. As he sat down on the bed beside her, she reached out for him. He took her in his arms, saying, 'I know, Mary, I know.'

It was all he said, as he held the widow of the man he reckoned to be the one true friend he'd ever known. Not many hours later, he looked down upon her as she lay deeply asleep. Before the sun was properly up, he promised himself, her problems would be over.

Sheriff Kincaid was at his desk rousing himself

from sleep when John Thirsk stepped into his
office at the pre-arranged time. While he collected
himself, John Thirsk helped himself to some
coffee from a pot that was keeping warm on a
stove. The two men said nothing to one another.
When they were both ready they left the office to
get their horses. As they rode out of town a short
while later, they were joined by Jesse. Neither
man said anything to the boy. It would have been
futile to try and stop him riding along with them.
It had, they knew, always been his fight, no
matter how much it had also become theirs.

They rode hard and fast to the Bar-X. Their way
was lighted by the rising sun. Without being told,
Jesse somehow knew what they were riding to do.
Milton was at breakfast by the time they reached
his sprawling acres. Without stopping, they rode
through the gates of the home place and had
dismounted their horses before two men who
were standing guard on the steps of Milton's big
house knew what had hit them. Hearing shots
Milton, who was sitting down to breakfast at the
head of a long table in his dining-room, stopped
mid-chew. By the time John Thirsk, Pat Kincaid
and Jesse Butler burst in on him he was standing
armed with a rifle. On seeing the number of guns
he was up against, he hesitated to open fire.

'Milton, you're under arrest,' Sheriff Kincaid
said to him, his Colt .45 drawn and pointing
straight at Milton.

The first thing that caught Milton's eye was the deputy badge on Thirsk's chest.

'This is good!' Milton barked in reply, pointing the barrel of his rifle in Thirsk's direction. 'He commits most of the murders round here, and you make him a deputy!'

'You're wasting your time,' Kincaid said. 'Now put down your rifle and come quietly, Milton. It's over.'

'What's over?' Milton asked. 'You don't know what you're talking about, Kincaid. You wouldn't even be here if Johnstone hadn't fetched you from Paragould. You don't know anything about what's been going on around here.'

'He knows enough.' Thirsk said between gritted teeth, all the hatred he'd ever felt for men like Milton welling up inside him. 'It may not have been what you intended when you appointed him sheriff, but he's the law now and you're under arrest.'

Just as he finished what he was saying, a man who'd been creeping around the side of the house suddenly jumped up at a window and, smashing the pane of glass, started firing, winging Jesse in his right arm. In a flash Kincaid returned fire and the man was sent reeling. Milton closed a finger on the trigger of his rifle but was gunned down by Thirsk. As Milton lay dying, blood gushing from a stomach wound, Thirsk turned his attention to Jesse.

'You all right, Jesse?' he asked, relieved to see he was still standing.

'Yeah, John,' replied Jesse, between snatches of caught breath. 'I'm just winged.'

Thirsk turned in time to see Milton breathe his last. He guessed he had known from the start that it was going to be Milton or him. He was just glad that when his end came Milton had seen it was at the hands of the law.

There was a panic in Lawrence County amongst the men in high places whom Milton had bought and stuffed in his pockets. Solomon Mayer was not one of them though. Telegrams had gone between him and Milton's next of kin in the East. It seemed the only next of kin Milton had was an uncle on his father's side. Solomon Mayer wrote him of the hell Milton had put the small settlers in the county through. Instructions had come back by return dismissing Milton's lawyer and appointing Mayer in his place. Further instructions said that he was to sell everything and drop all unresolved legal matters. It seemed someone else in that family had running in their veins the same blood that had made Milton's father so beloved and respected by the likes of Daniel Foster.

Under the protection of Pat Kincaid, its new marshal, Walnut Ridge was already settling into a more peaceful mode as, less than a week after swearing a deputy's oath, Thirsk mounted his horse in readiness to depart Horseshoe Farm and Arkansas.

'John, how can we ever thank you?' Mary asked.

'You don't have to, Mary,' Thirsk replied. 'Frank would have done the same for me. I was only doing what I had to.'

And so saying, he turned his horse and with a touch of his hat rode out of town.